END
OF THE
GUN

Center Point
Large Print

Also by H. A. DeRosso and available from Center Point Large Print:

The Dark Brand
The Gun Trail

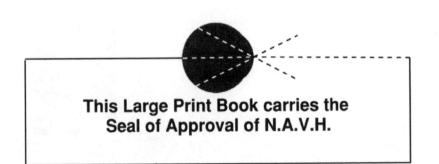

This Large Print Book carries the Seal of Approval of N.A.V.H.

END OF THE GUN

H. A. DeRosso

CENTER POINT LARGE PRINT
THORNDIKE, MAINE

This Center Point Large Print edition is published
in the year 2016 by arrangement with
Golden West Literary Agency.

First US edition: Permabooks.
First UK edition: Mills and Boon.

The text of this Large Print edition is unabridged.
In other aspects, this book may vary
from the original edition.
Printed in the United States of America
on permanent paper.
Set in 16-point Times New Roman type.

ISBN: 978-1-62899-944-0 (hardcover)
ISBN: 978-1-62899-948-8 (paperback)

Library of Congress Cataloging-in-Publication Data

Names: DeRosso, H. A. (Henry Andrew), 1917–1960, author.
Title: End of the gun / H. A. DeRosso.
Description: Center Point Large Print edition. | Thorndike, Maine :
Center Point Large Print, 2016. | ©1955
Identifiers: LCCN 2016002577 | ISBN 9781628999440
    (hardcover : alk. paper)
Subjects: LCSH: Large type books. | GSAFD: Western stories.
Classification: LCC PS3507.E695 E53 2016 | DDC 813/.54—dc23
LC record available at http://lccn.loc.gov/2016002577

For M. F.

1

In the pines, Britton waited patiently, peering steadily at the band of mustangs drinking at the spring below. The stallion was a coyote-dun with a black mane and tail and he kept moving about restlessly and warily, head flung up as he sniffed the air. Britton, however, was down-wind and he knew the stallion would never catch his scent.

The mares and colts drank thirstily and Britton made no move to interrupt them, for horses could not run at full speed when logged down with water. The coyote-dun would duck his head now and then for a few gulps. Then he would fling it up, ears cocked, snorting softly as he scanned the country for peril to his band.

Under Britton, the blaze-faced black shifted slightly and Britton moved effortlessly with it so that saddle leather would not creak. He kept half a glance on the black's muzzle, prepared to stifle any attempt the horse might make to whinny. The black flicked its tail occasionally as though impatient to be off but Britton held it in with a firm though gentle pull on the lines.

Despite his outward passiveness, Britton was aware of the quickened beating of his heart and of the surge of excitement in his blood. Perhaps this was the beginning of it, he thought, the beginning of everything he had dreamed of and yearned for those lonely, remorseful years.

He shifted his glance once to the country ahead, thinking as he did so of Kyle Reeve and Eddie Lane at their posts. A moment of misgiving descended on Britton as he dwelt on Reeve. Then, irritably, he shrugged the sensation from him and went on studying the land.

Beyond the spring, the land funneled into a winding draw. This was lonesome country here, high and rather arid, with the mountain peaks rising ragged and cruel. Pines and junipers grew in the lower elevations but the mountain crests were barren.

Returning his attention to the mustangs, Britton saw that several of them had already drunk their fill. They had begun to nibble at the grass which grew adjacent to the water hole. The stallion had his head down once more and was drinking deeply.

Now that the moment was at hand, Britton felt his heart quicken still more. Strain and excitement pulled his lips tight as he drew his .44. He waited while the stallion lifted his muzzle from the water and looked around, pawing nervously at the ground. All the mares and colts were done drinking now.

Britton swallowed, the walls of his throat constricting dryly. He tipped the six-shooter at the sky and, jabbing the black with the spurs, jumped it out into the open. He fired as he emerged from the pines and the sound of the shot brought the coyote-dun wheeling around, squealing in fright and alarm.

An instant the stallion appeared to freeze there, head high, ears cocked, distended eyes watching Britton come pounding down the slope. As Britton let loose with a shrill rebel yell and fired again, the stallion spun away. He squealed again, in rage and urgency, and nipped at the flanks of two mares nearby. With a rush and thunder of sound, the band took off.

They had no way to go but into the draw and Britton rushed them there. Their racing hoofs raised a great cloud of dust that almost obliterated them from sight. Britton roared into it. Through the roiling swirls, he could see the coyote-dun working hard at the rear of his band, nipping and biting and crowding to get all the speed he could out of his mares, but the water had loaded them down. The black was running easily, keeping up with the band without exerting itself, and exultation swept through Britton.

Dust worked up into his nostrils, the taste of it was in his mouth. He regretted now that he had not knotted a bandanna over his lips, but he was not going to take the time to do it. Something about the running horses, the feral beauty and primal quality of it, worked into Britton's blood and he had to give out with another yell of exuberance.

The black crowded close to the coyote-dun who was still doing his utmost to urge more speed out of his *manada*. The stallion could have outdistanced the mares and colts, but it was not in his wild nature to abandon his band. He snorted and squealed and bit and butted, but to no avail. The mustangs had all drunk too deeply.

The band roared out of the draw into open country. Britton reared up in the stirrups, anxiously searching the land through the spumes of dust that swirled and boiled. The band started to veer to the left and Britton swore. Damn you, Kyle, where are you?

He jabbed the black with the spurs and the horse responded with a rush of swiftness that carried it to the flank of the veering mustangs. Britton laid a shot alongside them, but in all the uproar the sound was dull and scarcely audible. The mustangs thundered on, still veering away.

Britton swore again. Rage rose and stormed in him. Where the hell are you, Kyle? You no-good, lazy son, where are you?

He lifted his head and looked about him, seeking Kyle Reeve, but the dust boiled so high and thick he could not see far. The herd was still swinging to the left, away from the canyon where the trap lay. Britton began to curse Reeve again, bitterly, savagely.

Then, when the rage was the darkest and most vicious in him, Britton heard Reeve's shouts. Damn you, Kyle, it's about time, thought Britton. Up ahead, through the dust, he saw Reeve racing in, yipping his rebel yell and swinging a blanket over his head. With a suddenness that was startling, the leading mares swerved to the right and the rest of the band followed. Britton dropped back until the black was running behind the band once more.

The coyote-dun swerved once, angling for the black with teeth bared and ears laid back. The stallion made a pass at Britton's thigh and he had to pull the black aside sharply and chop down with the barrel of his six-shooter. The coyote-dun squealed with pain as the gun cracked him across the muzzle. The click of his teeth as they closed made a distinct, savage sound. Britton chopped down again, hard, and the irate stallion screamed and wheeled away. It looked like he was going to desert the band, but then he took a vicious nip at the rump of a grulla mare that was starting to lag and with his front shoulders crowded her up with the rest of the band.

The *manada* started to swing to the right now but they did not move very far. Through the tumult of the running horses there came the shrill cries of Eddie Lane. Slitting his eyes against the boiling dust, Britton made out the boy up ahead, riding hunched over in the saddle of his sorrel and waving his blanket every time the mustangs tried to veer from their path.

In the wake of the band the dust at times was so thick that it stuck in Britton's throat stranglingly. His face was white, the dust lay so heavily on it. He could feel grit between his teeth. His eyes stung. He sputtered and choked and tried to spit and all that got him was more dust in his throat. Nevertheless, he threw back his head and let go another yell and then laughed in elation.

They had them now, Britton exulted, they had their first horses. The mouth of the canyon was no more than a mile ahead and once the mustangs were in there that would be the beginning of his dream. At this moment he knew so much joy that it became almost insufferable. His eyes were stinging again, but not so much from the dust as from sheer exhilaration.

The mustangs thundered on. The coyote-dun snorted and squealed and once when he bit the flank of a chestnut mare he took hide and hair right off, leaving the flesh raw and bare from which blood began to run. But the water-logged mustangs could move no faster and the riders on either side of them and Britton in the rear kept pace with them easily.

The first hint Britton got of anything wrong was Eddie Lane's strident shout. The boy was yelling something which Britton could not make out and he reared up in the stirrups in an attempt to see, but the swirling dust did not permit him to look very far. A gun blasted from ahead of the racing mustangs.

Britton swore and peered with narrowed eyes at Kyle Reeve there to the left. Reeve was in a position to see in front of the mustangs and he, too, was shouting and waving his blanket angrily. The gun ahead roared again, three fast shots this time, and Britton sensed the mustangs quiver with confusion.

The running horses appeared to suspend their motion for an instant as if poising for a change of direction. The gun boomed again, its sound mingled with Lane's irate shouting. Then the mustangs broke.

They scattered in all directions as the gun barked again. Britton saw five of them wheel and bear down on him, hoofs thrashing madly, nostrils distended as they snorted their uncertainty and panic. He threw a shot at the ground in front of the five mustangs, but this only split them. Three of them passed him on one side, two on the other. One of them raced by so close he could have reached out and touched its mane.

He saw another group break away and he jumped the black at them in an effort to turn them back, but the stallion, sensing his opportunity, wheeled suddenly and smashed into the black. The horse shuddered under Britton. Its stride broke and abruptly it went down on its front knees. Teeth bared, the coyote-dun snapped at Britton's arm and he had to lurch sideways violently to evade the teeth. Then the coyote-dun trumpeted a defiant cry and spun away.

Cursing savagely, Britton pulled the black to its feet and plunged it through the cloud of dust which was now settling a little. He made out Kyle Reeve as he started after several mustangs, but they had a head start and were scattering and he would never turn them back. Lane's high-pitched shouting was coming from ahead and Britton started toward the boy.

Britton passed a hand angrily over his stinging eyes and rode through the settling dust to where Eddie Lane was pulling up his sorrel in front of two riders. The boy was so full of anger he was trembling.

"What's the big idea of doing a thing like that?" Lane was shouting, face taut with wrath. "Tell me. What the hell's the big idea?"

The two riders turned their mounts so that they faced the boy. One of them, a big, dark, good-looking fellow, had a six-shooter in his hand. Apparently, he was the one who had done the shooting that had dispersed the mustangs. With a start, Britton saw that the other was a woman.

Britton slowed his black to a walk and rode up. Rage was a blaze in his brain. He looked off at the mouth of the box canyon which was their trap and his wrath heightened. Another quarter mile and the mustangs would have been in that canyon. Instead they were scattered all to hell and gone. Britton swore silently and reined in.

The man with the gun punched the spent shells out of his six-shooter. Then he reloaded, thumbing .45's out of his belt and inserting them in the cylinder with a deliberateness that had a touch of insolence to it. Lane saw and his face turned pink under its layer of dust.

"Answer me," the boy cried, sending his horse ahead so that it crowded against the big man's mount. "Damn you, answer me!"

The man looked up with a flash of resentment. He had finished reloading and now he hefted the six-shooter in his hand as though he were debating whether to use it. Britton still had his .44 in his fist and he laid the long barrel of the Colt on the saddle horn and aimed the .44 at the big man.

"Put up that six-shooter, bucko," said Britton. "Put it up fast or take a slug in the belly. It doesn't make any difference to me which you choose."

The big man turned a baleful glance on Britton. One corner of the man's mouth turned down in an expression of arrogance and contempt. Then he got another look at Britton's gray eyes and the big man grew suddenly wary. He holstered his weapon, doing it slowly but with that touch of insolence that seemed to be about everything he performed.

Britton took a deep breath. It stilled some of the wrath in him although its force was still strong and almost insufferable in his chest. "What's your name, bucko?" he asked.

"Rambone. Dick Rambone." The fellow had a deep yet soft voice. It held the purring quality of a truculent puma.

Britton glanced at the brand on Rambone's horse. "Chain Link," Britton translated softly. He raised his eyes back to Rambone's face. There appeared to be something sinistrous in Rambone's long, hooked nose and in the thin, wide pattern of his mouth. "What's your connection with Chain Link?"

"I'm ramrod of Chain Link."

Britton's eyes narrowed. His lips felt dry and cracking. The taste of dust was still in his mouth. "What was the idea of stampeding those mustangs?"

"I had no choice."

"What do you mean?"

"They were on me so fast I had to stampede them or be run down."

"That's a damn lie," cried Eddie Lane. He had reined his sorrel to the side. The boy was bent forward in the saddle, irate eyes fixed on Rambone's face. "You could have got out of the way easy."

Rambone turned a slow and insolent glance on Lane. The corners of Rambone's mouth pulled

16

in. "Careful who you call a liar, kid," he said, in a tone low and cold with menace. "Your partner's got a gun on me right now but there will be other times."

"I ain't scared," Lane declared hotly. "Put up your iron, Steve. I ain't scared of this hombre."

"Easy, Eddie," said Britton. He went on staring at Rambone and the rigidness of this finally pulled Rambone's glance off the boy and back to Britton. Rambone's eyes seemed to glaze over. "There was no reason why you couldn't see the horses coming," Britton went on. "They were making enough noise. Still you rode right into their way and stampeded them. We put in a lot of work on those horses, bucko."

Rambone's mouth showed a hint of contempt and indifference. "That's tough, hombre," he murmured.

Wrath swelled in Britton, he could feel its insistent ache behind his eyes. With an effort, he restrained himself. Nevertheless, his knuckles turned white from the force of his grip on the .44. "Don't crowd your luck, Rambone," he growled. "Don't crowd it at all."

Rambone took another careful consideration of Britton's tense face. Wariness and a studied speculation entered the Chain Link foreman's glance. When he spoke, his tone was rather placating.

"Maybe I could have ridden out of it," Rambone

said, and then nodded at the girl on the palomino beside him, "but I had Miss Hepburn to think about. That's why I stampeded those mustangs." His lips tightened. "Under the same circumstances I'd do it again."

As Britton turned his eyes on the girl, he was aware of Kyle Reeve riding up but Britton did not look at his partner. He heard Reeve rein in with a jingle of bit chains and a squealing of saddle leather. Reeve's bay coughed once, then there was silence.

The girl met Britton's glance at first, then her eyes wavered and dropped. She was a pretty one, Britton thought, with her blond hair done up in a ball and tied with a blue ribbon on the nape of her neck. Her brows were dark and her nose had a tilt to its tip and there was a cleft in her chin. She was wearing a divided skirt, fringed at the hem, and she sat the palomino astride with all the grace and ease of a born rider.

Something constricted in Britton's throat as he stared at her. For a moment words would not come to him. He had a fleeting remembrance of the past that left him strangely sad and shamed. Then he put the feeling from him.

He returned his glance to Rambone. "What're you doing here?"

"I could ask you the same thing," said Rambone.

The line of Britton's jaw turned hard. "This isn't Chain Link. You've got no business here."

"No?" drawled Rambone. One brow lifted archly. "I suppose you own the land here? I don't see any 'No Trespassing' signs."

Wrath surged in Britton again. He did not know how long he could contain it and he did not want trouble. With what lay behind him, he didn't want any trouble at all. He took a deep breath before he spoke.

"We're hunting mustangs here," he said. "We checked in Cordova before coming here and this is free range. All these mountains are free range. Chain Link doesn't reach to here. You've got no business interfering with us."

Rambone shrugged. "We weren't interfering. Those horses came on us so fast I had to stampede them. Like I told you, I had no choice."

"All right," said Britton, eyes slitted. He jumped the black ahead a step, then reined it in sharply. Everything in him shouted to smash the horse into Rambone's buckskin and send him hurtling out of the saddle. The skin drew tight over Britton's high cheekbones. "Maybe someday if me and my partners are riding along and we come across a herd of Chain Link cattle being driven, we'll take the easy way and stampede them instead of riding out of their path. How would you like that, Rambone?"

Rambone's eyes brightened. "You just try it, hombre," he said in a low, hard tone. "You just try it."

"Please, Dick," the girl said. It was the first time she had spoken and Britton felt his eyes pull back to her. She had a soft, pleasant voice, like the wind murmuring in the tops of pines. Her face looked strained and troubled. Her glance sought Britton's face, wavered once, then returned to stay. "We're sorry," she said to Britton. "It was all our fault. We assure you—"

"Stella!" Rambone said sharply, and the girl stopped abruptly. It seemed to Britton that she almost winced. "We don't have to apologize to these greasy-sack mustangers," said Rambone, voice heavy with contempt. His arrogant glance swept Britton with an almost palpable impact. "You watch your step, hombre. You're not far from Chain Link's line. I'll be riding by here again and you just be sure you watch your step."

"What do you mean by that?" growled Britton.

"Sometimes Chain Link's cows stray. Don't you or your partners encourage any straying."

Before Britton could answer, Kyle Reeve laughed softly and said, "Listen to the man. Why, to hear him talk anyone would think you were a crook, Steve."

A rush of blood filled Britton's face before he could check himself. Then the anger came. Damn you, Kyle, he thought, damn your careless, irresponsible heart. He was so full of wrath and consternation he could not think of anything to say.

Rambone lifted that brow again and stared at Britton's Colt, which was still in his hand. "We'll be riding on now," said Rambone. "Come, Stella."

They rode off, ignoring Britton's .44. He was hardly aware that he was still holding it. All that his mind comprehended was a deep sense of humiliation and regret. His eyes stared straight ahead without seeing anything. After a while, he realized that Eddie Lane was watching him closely and this roused Britton. He holstered the six-shooter and glanced at Kyle Reeve.

Reeve had turned his bay so that he could observe Rambone and the girl riding away. Under the tawny mustache, there was a slanted smile on Reeve's mouth. An avid glitter brightened his yellow eyes.

"Mighty purty filly," he murmured. "Yes, sir! A mighty purty filly, Steve."

Steve Britton said nothing. He sat there in his saddle, listening to the measured, lonely beating of his heart. . . .

2

Britton crouched in front of the fire, slicing potatoes into the kettle. Wood smoke kept swirling up, stinging his eyes even though he kept them slitted. A cigarette drooped out of a corner of his wide mouth, but the smoke had gone out. Britton did not bother to light it again. He was thinking.

The trend of his thoughts left its grave and solemn mark on his face. Tiny crevices edged the corners of his squinted eyes and the ends of his mouth. Below his high cheekbones the planes of his face were gaunt and sunken, giving him a look of hunger. He had not shaved in two days and a black beard stubble lined his face and the front of his neck.

Eddie Lane walked up with an armful of dried piñon. He dropped the wood with a clatter on the pile beside the fire. Then Lane brushed bits of wood dust from his sleeves and shirt front and peered out into the gathering twilight.

"When the hell is Kyle coming in?" asked the boy. His tone was sharp with irritation.

"He rode out to see where those mustangs went to," said Britton, without looking up.

"Well, it shouldn't take him this long."

"They might have drifted a long way, Eddie."

The boy snorted. He was tall and slim but the promise of bigness lay in the spread of his shoulders. He gave them a nettled shrug.

"Seems to me he's always riding out around suppertime. Gives him an excuse not to help out with the chores."

Britton said nothing. He poured a little water into the kettle, then went back to slicing potatoes. He could feel the boy's eyes on him, solemn and thoughtful.

"How come you teamed up with Kyle, Steve?" Lane asked, after a while.

"I've known him a long time," Britton said softly.

Lane thought on this a while. If he reached any conclusion, he kept it to himself. He went on staring at Britton. Finally, he said, "You need anything else, Steve?"

"No thanks, Eddie."

The boy turned and walked off. Britton threw him a look. Lane was nineteen and like Britton the boy had a dream. Perhaps this was why they were so close, Britton thought. Two lonely men with only a dream to sustain them. The only difference between them was that Lane had nothing to remember. Britton's lips tightened. It was no good always thinking like this, he told himself, but the memory was so vivid and painful he could not help it.

Lane went into the lean-to they had constructed

here in the box canyon and came out with his guitar. He seated himself on a rock and for a while he strummed soft, sad chords. Then he began to sing.

"As I walked out in the streets of Laredo,
As I walked out in Laredo one day,
I spied a poor cowboy wrapped up in white
    linen,
Wrapped up in white linen and cold as the
    day . . ."

Britton sliced the last potato and put the lid on the kettle. He rose to his feet; a tall, dark man with brooding gray eyes and the shadow of disillusionment in the lines about his mouth. He stood there, motionless, listening.

" 'I see by your outfit that you are a cowboy,'
These words he did say as I boldly stepped by.
'Come sit down beside me and hear my sad
    story;
I was shot in the breast and I know I must
    die . . .' "

A pine knot exploded with a sound as sharp as a gunshot. Somewhere in the gathering dusk an owl hooted and something passed overhead on whispering wings. The wind moaned a little as it came down the canyon.

" 'Let sixteen gamblers come handle my
   coffin,
Let sixteen cowboys come sing me a song,
Take me to the graveyard and lay the sod o'er
   me,
For I'm a poor cowboy and I know I've done
   wrong . . .' "

Britton bent down and picked up a brand from
the fire and lighted his dead cigarette. He
inhaled deeply and before his eyes, poignantly,
there drifted the image of the blond girl he had
seen with Rambone that day. It was visions like
these that heightened Britton's loneliness until,
at times, it was almost unbearable. They made
him remember those days and nights when the
dream had been all that had kept him from
weeping with hopelessness and despair. He
started to wonder if he would ever come to
know a good woman.

" 'It was once in the saddle I used to go
   dashing,
It was once in the saddle I used to go gay.
'Twas first to drinking and then to card
   playing,
Got shot in the breast and I'm dying today . . .' "

Britton stared down at the fire, for the moment
lost in contemplation of his dream. There was a

woman in it, a woman he had never met and most likely never would, but there was a ranch in the dream, too, a place of his own. This last he would have, he promised himself fiercely. This last he would have despite everything.

" 'Get six jolly cowboys to carry my coffin,
Get six pretty girls to carry my pall;
Put bunches of roses all over my coffin,
Put roses to deaden the clods as they fall . . .' "

From out of the dusk came the sounds of a running horse. Britton's head lifted and his eyes squinted as he peered. A rider materialized out of the shadows, coming in fast. It was Kyle Reeve.

" 'Oh beat the drum slowly and play the fife
lowly
And play the dead march as you carry me
along,
Take me to the green valley and lay the sod
o'er me,
For I'm a young cowboy and I know I've
done wrong . . .' "

Reeve reined his bay to a sliding halt down by one of the corrals they had thrown up. He stripped off saddle and bridle and turned the animal into the enclosure. Then he came up to the fire, his fancy Mexican spurs singing shrilly.

He bent over the kettle and lifted the lid and made a face after he had inhaled. "Stew again?" he said, his voice disgusted.

"If you don't like the grub," Britton said quietly, "you can always cook your own."

Reeve replaced the lid and straightened. In the firelight his face looked rugged and handsome. The tawny mustache dropped down around the corners of his mouth and now he raised a hand and touched the mustache and then his silky sideburns while his eyes studied Britton. After a moment, Reeve's teeth flashed white as he smiled.

"I was only joking, Stevie. You're a hell of a good cook. Much better than me and the kid, anyway. Make some girl a good husband you would. Wouldn't he, kid?"

The boy did not speak. He had stopped singing. He sat there on the rock, strumming the guitar idly and softly, eyes fixed on Reeve.

"See anything, Kyle?" asked Britton.

Reeve shrugged. He turned, putting himself sideways to the fire, and the light of it glinted redly off the silver discs in a row down his bat-wing chaps. "I'll bet they didn't stop running until they got to the other side of the Ladrones. We're gonna have a hell of a time getting our hands on that bunch again. Damn that Rambone anyway."

Britton's cigarette was down to a butt and he

flipped this into the fire. He stood there, staring moodily at the flames.

"Say," said Reeve, as the thought suddenly hit him, "that Hepburn filly is pretty nice, isn't she?"

Britton said nothing. He kept looking at the fire. Mention of the girl had brought her picture vividly to his mind and he felt a tiny ache lodge in his throat.

"Hepburn," Reeve said musingly, frowning as though he were immersed in thought. "Isn't that the family that owns Chain Link? Say, she wouldn't be a bad catch. I heard in Cordova that Chain Link is the biggest spread in these parts." His eyes searched Britton again. "Didn't you notice that filly, Steve?"

"I saw her," said Britton. His voice sounded gruff and thick and alien to his ears. He bent down and lifted the lid from the kettle. "Chow's ready," he said.

Reeve grabbed a tin plate and filled it to the brim with stew. He sat down on a rock nearby and began to eat with gusto. Eddie Lane laid his guitar on the ground and walked over and waited while Britton helped himself. Then the boy ladled some stew into his own plate.

They ate in silence. Reeve had a second helping, as generous as the first. Britton saw Lane throw a disapproving look at Reeve. On the instant, the boy appeared as though he were going to say something, but then he shrugged and went back to eating.

When Reeve was through, he exhaled loudly and rose to his feet. He slapped his stomach contentedly and said, "Well, I'll go take a look at the horses." He burped and started for the corral.

Lane watched him go. The boy's thin face was marked with disgust and resentment. "Look at him," he growled in a low voice. "He don't give a damn about the horses except when there's the dishes to be washed."

Britton said nothing. He wiped his mouth with the back of his hand and then he rose to his feet and picked up Reeve's plate and spoon where they had been dropped carelessly on the ground. When Britton straightened, Lane was there, his hand outstretched.

"You do the cooking, I do the washing. Fair enough?" said the boy, and grinned.

Something warm stirred in Britton and he smiled in return. He could not remember the last time he had smiled, but then there had been so little to smile about for years and there had been no one he had really liked until he had met this boy and they had thrown in as partners to hunt mustangs.

"All right, Eddie."

The boy carried the kettle and the plates over to the spring nearby which was the reason the partners had selected this canyon for their camp.

Britton went into the lean-to and came out with his bedroll. He spread the blankets and then he got his saddle and placed it at the head of the roll to serve as his pillow. After that, he sat down on the kack and built a cigarette.

It was night now. Somewhere a coyote began to cry. Overhead the stars glittered brightly, like shining pinpoints of steel. Down by the corral something tiny glowed red briefly as though Reeve were drawing on a smoke. One of the horses snorted fretfully and the coyote called again. Then there was silence.

Eddie Lane came back from the spring and put the kettle and plates away. Then he poured himself another cup of coffee from the pot which was still on the fire. He carried the cup over to his rock and set it down beside him and picked up his guitar. He started to strum and hum softly.

The singing of Reeve's spurs preceded him back to the fire. He, too, poured himself another cup of coffee. He sipped it and exhaled his pleasure audibly and then went over and sat down on his bedroll, holding the cup in both hands between his legs.

"Yes, sir," said Reeve, "that Hepburn filly is real nice. Sure could have myself a time if she was here right now. Yes, sir!"

Lane struck a loud, angry chord on the guitar. "Don't you talk like that about her, Kyle. She's a nice girl."

Reeve turned his head indolently and stared at Lane. "There's no such thing as a nice girl, kid. All women are chippies at heart."

"Don't you say that. Some of them might be but not all of them. Not Miss Hepburn anyway. Not my Mona, either."

"Your Mona," Reeve murmured. He sounded amused. "What do you think your Mona is doing right now, Eddie?"

"My Mona's waiting for me," the boy said, a measure of defiance in his tone. "When I left Palo Pinto she said she'd wait until I got back and she will, too. There was nothing around Palo Pinto for me and I left to see if I couldn't get a stake so we could get married. That's why I drifted here to New Mexico. My Mona will wait for me no matter how long it takes."

"Sure, kid, sure," Reeve said soothingly. He lifted a hand and caressed his sideburns. His chuckle made a soft sound in the night. "She'll be in Palo Pinto when you get back, all right. I won't argue that. But what do you think she'll be doing in the meantime? It's only natural for her to want a little fun."

Lane laid the guitar flat in his lap and leaned forward. Firelight reflected off the taut high points of his cheeks. "Watch what you say about Mona, Kyle. Watch it."

Reeve chuckled again. "I'm just telling you how it is, Eddie. I've been around and, believe me, I know women. I'm really telling you this for your own good. You're young, Eddie, and you've got a lot of silly, noble ideas about women, but the day will come when you'll see that I'm right. Women are all alike."

"Maybe the kind of women you go for, Kyle," the boy declared, voice thick with resentment and indignation, "but there are other kinds too. My Mona is a nice girl and so is Stella Hepburn."

"All right, kid, all right," said Reeve, holding up a hand. "Don't get your hackles up. But I still say there isn't a woman who doesn't like a little fun and that goes for the Hepburn filly and your Mona too."

The strings of the guitar hummed resoundingly as it hit the ground. Lane was on his feet, face contorted angrily. "Damn you, Kyle, you ain't saying things like that about Mona!"

Britton jumped to his feet. Two quick steps placed him between Reeve and Lane. Lane started to lunge ahead, but Britton grabbed him by the arms, restraining him. Britton's glance was hot and wrathful on Kyle Reeve.

"Will you keep your big mouth shut, Kyle?" growled Britton, voice aquiver with fury.

Lane kept trying to get around Britton but Britton held him back. The boy was sobbing with rage. "He's got no call to talk like that," he kept saying. "He's got no call to talk like that about my Mona."

A look of mock innocence distorted Reeve's face. "Did I say anything wrong, Steve? Hell, I was just making conversation. Is there anything wrong in saying that I'd like to have myself a time with the Hepburn filly? Don't you feel the same way?"

"You talk about her like that again, Kyle," said Britton, "and I'll kill you!"

"Oh?" said Reeve, his brows going up. His eyes took on a calculating gleam as he stared searchingly at Britton. "Oh?" Reeve said again. "It's like that, is it?"

"You heard me, Kyle."

Reeve's face turned bland and expression-less. His eyes held a glittering opacity. "I heard you."

Lane gave a violent wrench and this time he broke loose from Britton's grip. As the boy passed him, Britton leaped, grabbing Lane about the shoulders. Lane shouted in anger and twisted violently in an attempt to break away again, but Britton held on. It took all his strength to wrestle the boy away from Reeve. Britton gave a savage wrench that spun the boy away and sent him stumbling to his knees. Lane came up instantly, however, cursing and sobbing with rage.

"All right," he cried, crouching, his hand poised over the handle of the .44 Remington he wore at his hip. "We'll have it out this way then. Reach, Kyle!"

Britton planted himself in front of the boy. "Cut it out, Eddie. It's all over. Kyle didn't mean anything. Tell him you didn't mean anything, Kyle."

Reeve had risen to his feet. He stood there, rather lax, but his right hand hung beside his holster, just below the pearl grip of his .45. "I don't have to tell him anything," Reeve said coldly. "I'll take him on any time he feels like it. I'll show the squirt."

Britton turned slowly, keeping himself in front of Lane all the while. "You'll tell him you're sorry, Kyle," Britton said through his teeth, "or you'll take both of us on together."

Reeve did not speak right away. His eyes narrowed and brightened; they searched Britton's face with a keen, hot intensity. One hand rose and brushed briefly against the tawny mustache. Reeve's chest swelled as he drew a prodigious breath. When he let it out, it made an audible sound.

"What's got into you, Steve? I was only joshing. Can't a man have a little fun?" he said quietly. The focus of his eyes shifted past Britton to where Lane stood, still crouched and ready. Reeve's lips curved in a slight grin. "All right, kid. I'm sorry. I was just riding you. You feel any better now?"

Lane uttered a choked sob. He straightened as the tenseness went out of him and he walked over and picked up his guitar. The sob sounded again as he went into the lean-to.

Once more Reeve laid that searching look on Britton. "You've really changed, haven't you?" said Reeve.

He bent down and started to unroll his blankets. . . .

The black pricked up its ears and this alerted Britton. He reined in and peered through the break in the pines and what he saw caused the breath to catch in his throat for an instant.

The stallion was grazing, totally unaware that anyone was watching. It was a magnificent animal, even at this distance, and Britton felt the blood race in his veins. He had covered much of the Ladrones, which was what this mountain range was called, but this was the first that he had seen of this animal.

Eyes squinting, Britton kneed the black ahead cautiously, studying the lay of the land. A sheer cliff reared just beyond the stallion and Britton was figuring if he could force the horse against this rampart so that it could not flee he might have an opportunity to rope it.

As the black moved slowly in at a walk, its hoofs soundless on the sandy earth, Britton got his rope and shook out a loop. His eyes never left the stallion.

The wind was in Britton's face and this carried

his scent away from the stallion, which still grazed, rump to Britton, black tail flicking every now and then. The sun was bright on the animal's hide and it shone blue-black in the glare. The horse moved on a couple of steps and Britton saw the sinuous rippling of tendons in its quarters. The breath was warm and tight in Britton's throat.

Then the black's shod hoofs struck a stone. The sound of this sent the stallion's head up high in a burst of surprise. It trumpeted once in alarm and terror and came wheeling around, wild eyes glaring.

Britton had already jabbed the black with the spurs. The horse broke into a swift run, closing in on the stallion, which wheeled to start in the other direction. Rising in the stirrups, Britton made a cast with the lariat but the stallion broke at the same time and the noose brushed harm-lessly down across its hind quarters.

The stallion trumpeted again and lunged off. Britton gathered in his rope, spurring the black all the while, and shook out another loop. He kept the black on the stallion's flank, thus forcing the animal against the foot of the cliff. Ahead a small cul-de-sac appeared in the wall of the cliff and it was Britton's intention to drive the stallion into this where it would be trapped.

They were almost there when the rider burst out of the crevice. He emerged so suddenly that the stallion snorted in panic and reared high, front legs pawing the air. Still rearing, the stallion wheeled, almost crashing into Britton and the black. Britton made a try with the rope, but the stallion was coming down then and the loop sailed futilely over its head.

The stallion snorted again, a sound of primal, brutish rage, and then it broke past Britton. Jerking on the lines, he spun the black, gathering in his rope, but the stallion was away from the cliff and streaking across open ground. The realization came to Britton that he would never catch it now.

Disgustedly, he pulled the running black down to a walk and then turned it and started back. He coiled his rope and hung it back on the horn. By then the anger was very strong in Steve Britton. It put pinpoints of brightness in his eyes and pinched in the corners of his mouth.

The rider had started to leave but Britton put spurs to the black and sent it at a gallop in pursuit. "Hey, you," he shouted. "Hold on there!"

The rider threw a frightened look over his shoulder and when he saw Britton bearing down on him at a swift run, the rider halted his roan and turned it so that he faced Britton. Britton pulled the black in to a sliding halt that sprayed sand and raised a small cloud of dust.

Wrath was hammering in Britton's temples. It blinded him to everything else. "What the hell was the idea of that?" he shouted, eyes glowering.

"You did it deliberately. You made me miss that horse deliberately."

The rider was a boy, even younger than Eddie Lane. The boy had a lean face burned red by the sun. He looked at Britton's raging features and swallowed, his blue eyes averted. He hung his head and said nothing.

"I'm getting damn sick and tired of everybody interfering," raged Britton. "Every time I'm ready to take a horse some son of a bitch comes and busts it up. I've had my fill of it. Why did you make me lose that horse, kid?"

The boy went on staring at the ground. "He's mine," he said. His voice was low and barely audible and it quavered a little. "Midnight's mine."

"Yours?" cried Britton. "I didn't see any brand on him. What do you mean yours?"

"I've been after him for a month," said the boy, still looking down. He was twisting the ends of the lines nervously about his fingers. "I've hounded him so much he's left his band. This is his favorite grazing place and I was waiting here for him. He'd have passed right in front of me and I'd have had him then." His head lifted suddenly in a show of defiance. "I was in that hole all morning, waiting. It's you who interfered with me, not the other way around," he said somewhat loudly, but his chin trembled and, after a moment, his glance fell.

Now that the anger was ebbing in Britton, it

came to him that there was something familiar about this boy. Not that he had ever seen the youth before. It was something other than that, something in the shape of the boy's face and the expensive texture of his clothes and in his hesitant, almost submissive manner. A thought occurred to Britton and he lowered his glance and read the brand on the roan. It was Chain Link.

"What's your name, son?" Britton asked, his tone controlled and soft now.

"Bob Hepburn."

"Do you have a sister?"

"Yes." The boy's eyes lifted and studied Britton with a patent interest. "Do you know her?"

Britton did not answer this. "Why do you want that horse?"

The boy hung his head. "I just want him, that's all." His tone was sullen.

"Are you hunting him alone?"

"Yes."

Britton shifted his weight in the saddle and glanced about him at the lonesomeness and bleakness of the land. The wrath was a thing of the past in him now. Something about this boy touched Britton. Everything lonely and forlorn touched him, it seemed. Perhaps this was because he himself had never known anything else.

"This is lonesome country, son," said Britton. "You should have someone with you."

"I'll manage."

"If you get hurt, there will be no one to look after you."

"I said I'll manage." The boy's tone was suddenly sharp. His chin came up, but he still would not look at Britton. The boy was staring off at the red, serrated face of the cliff.

Britton stifled a sigh. "Well, so long, son," he said, and turned the black away.

He had ridden only a short distance when he heard the boy start after him. Britton reined in the black and waited. Young Hepburn came up and stopped the roan beside Britton. An urgency burned in the boy's countenance and left a troubled look in his blue eyes.

Hepburn made as if to speak but his lips only moved. No sound emerged from them. He hung his head again.

"What is it, son?" Britton asked gently.

The boy kept on staring down at his hands around which the ends of the lines were wrapped tightly. His mouth grew taut as if he were suddenly angry and disgusted with himself. His head snapped up and for an instant his eyes were bright with defiance and purpose.

"I want Midnight," he cried, his voice rather shrill. "He's mine."

"I'd say he belongs to the first man to dab a loop on him," said Britton.

Beads of sweat popped out on young

Hepburn's brow. "He's mine, I tell you. You hear?"

"I'm a mustanger, son. Any horse running wild is fair game to me."

The boy tried to meet Britton's hard look with the directness of his own but his quickly wavered and then averted. Hepburn's shoulders slumped. A sound like a sob came out of him.

"Please," the boy begged. He kept his eyes downcast. Shame burned in the high color in the crests of his cheeks. "Please, mister. I want him. I need him. He's just another horse to you but to me he's everything. Please leave him to me. I'll pay you to leave him to me." He was almost crying.

A bit of distaste passed through Britton but the feeling of compassion quickly dispelled this. He reached out and put a hand on the boy's shoulder. Britton's voice was soft when he spoke.

"You can buy certain things, son, but they'll never mean half as much as if you'd really earned them. You don't want to *buy* Midnight, do you? If it was only a question of buying a horse, you could buy much finer ones than Midnight. Isn't that right?"

The boy's head lifted slowly and the look he laid on Britton was almost timid. The boy's lips were pale, they moved stiffly when he spoke. "I've just *got* to have him," he whispered. "Don't you under-stand? I've just *got* to."

"I think I do," Britton said quietly. He showed the boy a faint smile and slapped his shoulder lightly. "You just stick to it, son. You'll get Midnight."

The boy's face lit up. "You mean you're leaving him to me?" he cried.

Britton's features turned stern. "No one's leaving him to you. You've just got to show you're the better man by dabbing your loop on him first." His eyes probed the boy's face. "Isn't that how you want it?"

"Sure," the boy whispered. He licked his lips and something fierce glowed in his eyes for an instant. "That's how it's going to be too. You just watch and see. . . ."

3

They fenced off every water hole and spring within miles of the box canyon except one, so that the mustangs had nowhere else to drink in that vicinity. Then they waited. For several days no horses used this water hole. It was almost as if they sensed that something was wrong.

Britton spied several *manadas*, but none of them would approach the water. One day, however, a band belonging to a grulla picked up the scent of the water and headed toward it. The mares and colts appeared eager to drink but the grulla stallion kept prancing around and sniffing the air and when the *manada* was almost at the water's edge some feral instinct alarmed the grulla. He trumpeted a cry of warning and fright and, nipping the mares nearest him, started the whole band off in panicked flight.

Britton and his partners avoided this spring for a few days in the hope that their absence might lure some *manadas* into using the water again. The partners patrolled the fenced-off springs instead, making sure that the fences and barriers were still in place. They found one water hole where the mustangs had managed to break through and they repaired the fence and then went on waiting.

One day they rode by the open water hole and saw in the evidence of hoofmarks and droppings on the sand that some mustangs had started using this spring again. They had drunk recently for the water was still muddy and it was a trait of mustangs that they liked to muddy a water hole before drinking. So the partners made plans for a run the following day.

They rode out at dawn and the sun was up when they took up their stations. Britton sat on the black in the pines again, waiting with an irritated impatience this day. He could not get the remembrance of the aborted run of the other day out of his mind and the recollection left him feeling nettled and ugly. He tried telling himself that a similar occurrence would not happen three times in succession, but he found small solace in the thought. The desire for the dream burned too brightly and urgently in him. His life held nothing else, nothing but loneliness and a shameful memory. If it were not for the dream, he would have long ago given way to despair.

In the middle of the morning the *manada* appeared over the rise and came trotting down to the spring. It was the grulla's band. They moved easily and readily this day with a minimum of suspicion. The grulla's wariness was nothing more than instinctive. He sniffed the air and pawed the ground lightly and pranced around the spring while his up-flung head surveyed the land about him but all this occurred because it was in his nature to do so. In a little while he was standing in the water, drinking with the mares and colts.

The mustangs were all filled with water, some of the mares and colts rolling on their backs and the others just beginning to graze, when Britton spurred the black out of the pines. The grulla's head snapped up, mane flapping, and he trumpeted an alarm. Biting and gouging and kicking, he started his *manada* in flight. Britton fired his .44 in a signal to Reeve and Lane that the run was under way and then he let loose with a yell and sent the *manada* stampeding into the draw.

He rode hard on the grulla's heels. Britton holstered his six-shooter and took his coiled rope in his right hand and once when the grulla swerved to take a bite at the black, Britton brought the coiled lariat down in a stinging blow on the stallion's muzzle. The grulla veered away and crowded up so hard against a white mare that she stumbled and almost went sprawling. But she regained her feet and then was running true again.

Dust stung Britton's eyes. This time, however, he had taken the precaution to knot a bandanna over his nose and mouth and he found breathing much easier and cleaner. He rode through the billowing dust, scarcely seeing where he was going, trusting to Reeve and Lane to point the mustangs right.

The earth seemed to tremble beneath the furious

pounding of the mustangs' panicked hoofs. The sound swelled upward, resounding from the sky. The hills and draws took up the din and hurled it rolling in booming echoes.

Above the thunder of the running horses, Britton could hear the shrill yipping of his partners. Now elation entered into the sounds and Britton felt his heart exult. Through the swirling, spuming dust he caught a glimpse of the walls that reared on either side of the canyon's mouth. His head dropped back and through the muffling bandanna he yipped his jubilation.

The *manada* sped into the canyon and past the partners' camp with Reeve and Lane on either side, steering it with blankets that flapped and furled in the wind stirred up by the running horses. Ahead lay the penning corral, built of stout, high poles laced together with rawhide and with a wing whose walls were camouflaged with brush extending in an ever-widening pattern away from the gate which was now open. The mustangs raced into this wing without hesitation and Reeve and Lane held back until all the horses were in and then, along with Britton, crowded the *manada* until every horse was in the corral.

Britton shut the gate and then all three of them sat there in their saddles, breathing hard while the sweat traced channels through the dust on their cheeks. They listened joyfully to the sounds of the mustangs milling in the corral and slamming up against its walls in insensate, baffled fury.

Britton pulled the bandanna down around his neck. He turned the black and started it at a walk for the camp. Reeve and Lane followed. The boy was laughing. He was trying to say something but the excitement was so great in him that only garbled laughter emerged.

Britton dismounted at the camp site and loosened the black's cinches. He started a fire and put the coffeepot on. Eddie Lane was grinning widely as he stepped down from his sorrel. Even Reeve looked pleased. His yellow eyes were bright with excitement and satisfaction.

"Well, that's the first of them, Stevie," Reeve exclaimed. "We're on our way."

"Nothing's gonna stop us now," the boy added happily, rubbing his hands together. He turned and threw a glance up the canyon and chuckled throatily.

Britton answered his partners' smiles with one of his own. He could not remember the last time he had felt as gay as right now and the thought made his eyes sting. He bent down and poked at the fire.

They waited until the coffee was ready and then each poured a cup. Lane took a swallow of his and said, "Man, this sure tastes good."

Reeve drank some of his and then swirled the rest in his cup while he stared down at it. "Sure could go for a slug of whiskey," he said. "Ain't had none for so long I've about forgot what it tastes like."

"You'll have plenty of time for whiskey drinking when this is over," said Britton.

"Yeah. But that's a long way off."

Britton looked at Reeve who was still staring down at his cup. Britton said, "You knew that when you threw in with us."

Reeve's head came up. On the moment his face was grave, then he flashed a smile, his teeth very white. "I'm not kicking. Now that we're getting somewhere, I'm not kicking a-tall."

Lane finished his coffee and turned to stare up the canyon again. "Where do we start, Steve?" he asked.

"We better cut out the culls first. No sense letting them use up graze and water."

"That's right," agreed Reeve. He swallowed the rest of his coffee and smacked his lips. "You and Eddie can handle that. Me, I'll go check up on the water holes and see can I spot some more mustangs."

Reeve swung up on his bay and rode off. Lane watched him go. The boy's hands were on his hips and his face was dark. He muttered a curse and said, "Is this how it's going to be all the time? Is he just going to keep on riding out when there's work to be done?"

"Skip it, Eddie."

The boy turned a burning glance on Britton. "We're partners, aren't we? Share and share alike, isn't that the agreement? Kyle's going to get just as much out of this as we are, isn't he? Then why the hell don't he share in the work?"

"He'll do his share. Kyle's a good man at breaking horses."

"Hah," said Lane. He spun on his heel and looked up the canyon once more. After a while, he said, subdued now, "How they look to you, Steve?"

Britton's brows knitted. "There's a few culls among them but you've got to expect that. Offhand I'd say there are at least a dozen in this bunch that'll make good horses, maybe three or four more."

The boy turned his head and stared inquiringly at Britton. "Do you think we'll make anything, Steve?"

"We won't get rich quick if that's what you mean."

"I don't want to get rich. I just want a little stake so I can marry Mona."

"You'll get it, Eddie. There's lots of mustangs in the Ladrones and we've just begun." Britton hitched up his belt. "Well, let's get started. . . ."

Britton and Lane started by walking round and round the outside of the corral to accustom the frenzied horses inside to their smell. The mustangs squealed and snorted and now and then some of them smashed up against the poles in a panicked effort to break through to freedom. The grulla tried several times to leap over the wall, but the poles were too high and each time he rebounded to come crashing down on his back.

Eventually, however, the mustangs quieted and then Britton and Lane got their horses and went to work. It was hot, dirty labor. The mustangs milled and whirled, raising spumes of dust that stuck to the partners' clothing and seeped into their eyes and noses. They roped the runts and led them, fighting and plunging, out of the canyon where they were released.

Britton was leading the last cull, a runty paint, when he spied the rider crossing the flat toward the canyon. Britton flipped his loop off the paint and yipped and the runt took off at a heel-kicking run to freedom. As he coiled his rope, Britton studied the rider. After a while, he made out the horse as a palomino.

Britton's heart skipped a beat and for a moment his throat went dry. He went on watching the rider who had by now spotted Britton and was angling directly at him. A vision of the old dream crossed Britton's mind almost tantalizingly, then was gone.

Stella Hepburn rode up and reined in just in front of Britton. Neither of them spoke right away. The girl stared at Britton solemnly and even a little fearfully. Britton's throat constricted as he looked at her.

That other time he had not paid too much attention to her because he had been so caught up with wrath and vexation. Now, however, he studied her out of slightly narrowed eyes. She was even prettier than he had remembered her, he thought. Her head was tilted back as she stared up at him and he could see the color of her eyes—a clear, startling blue.

She was wearing a bright red shirt and a fringed buckskin jacket and the same fringed, divided riding skirt. There was a fine layer of dust over this which indicated that she had come a long way, but she still looked fresh and clean.

As he stared at her, Britton became doubly conscious of his own soiled clothing and the sweat-streaked dust on his face and the black beard stubble that lent him a brooding and sinistrous look. He shifted uneasily in the kack and saddle leather squealed faintly. This seemed to rouse the girl.

"I want to tell you how sorry I am for the other day," she said in a humble tone. She stirred uncomfortably in her saddle and the focus of her eyes moved past him. "It—it was uncalled for, what we did. I'd like you to know how I feel."

"Thank you," said Britton. The words sounded rather thick in his ears and he wondered about that.

"It won't happen again."

"Forget it, I already have."

Her eyes came back to him. The evasiveness was gone from them, they looked warm and clear. "Isn't your name Britton?"

"That's right."

"I'm Stella Hepburn," she said, and surprised him by stretching out her hand. He took it with a feeling of faint embarrassment. Her fingers were long and slim and cool.

"Pleased to meet you, ma'am," he mumbled.

She withdrew her hand from his clasp. Her eyes dropped and she appeared to become lost in reflection. Her lips tightened and there was a graveness in the shape of her features. She was like that for a while. Then her eyes lifted.

"I wonder if you'd help me, Britton?" she said.

The question startled him a little. He could not make it out. "Ma'am?" he queried, puzzled.

A little color came into her face as though she were suddenly ill at ease. "It—it really isn't me," she said, shifting again in her saddle. "It would be more of a favor than anything else." Something desperate and appealing entered her eyes. "It's—it's my brother."

"Yes?" said Britton. He still could not figure anything out.

"Could you kind of look after him?"

Britton stared at her narrowly. "Why?"

She made a small, nervous gesture with her hand as if that were explanatory. Then she realized it wasn't and she pulled in her lower lip while she thought. Her eyes drifted from his face and became withdrawn and pensive.

"He's out here all alone," she said, anxiety in her voice. "I worry about him all the time. After all, he's just a boy."

"What's he doing up here?" asked Britton.

"He wants that wild horse he calls Midnight."

"I know that. Why does he want him?"

She drew a deep breath and held it while she stared into the distance. After a while, she exhaled and said, "I—I don't know if I can explain. I don't know if you'd understand. You see, Bob wants to prove himself. That's the best I can put it."

Britton said nothing. He sensed that she was not through, that more would follow, and he waited for her to proceed when she was ready.

After a pause, she went on, "It's—it's our father." Her head dropped and her whole bearing suggested shame and embarrassment at revealing something personal and intimate. "Father means well. Bob and I have everything we desire and we can't complain in that respect. I don't suppose it's Father's fault either because he had to be this way to get where he is. It's just that he's so—so domineering."

She paused again, face working as though she were searching for words. Britton said nothing. He sat there on the black and waited.

"Father is used to ordering everyone around,"

she continued, after a time. "He figures that someday Bob will run Chain Link and he wants Bob to be like him, but Bob just isn't built that way. This makes Father furious. About a month ago they had a terrible argument. Bob finally got so angry that he said he was through being bossed and dominated. Father told him he would never amount to anything, that he'd be a—a sniveling coward all his life. Bob left home then. He came here into the Ladrones and he set out to catch and break Midnight because no one's ever done that. He just wants to prove that he can do something on his own. He wants to prove he's a man in his own right."

Britton still said nothing. The girl was winding the ends of the lines about her fingers and it struck Britton how similar this was to what her brother had done that day.

"Won't you keep an eye on him, Britton?" she asked, face lifted up to him, a plea in her voice. "Won't you kind of look to see if he's all right every now and then? I ride out almost every day to see him. He won't let anyone else from Chain Link near him. Would you help him, Britton?"

"Why pick me?" Britton said slowly. "You don't know anything about me."

"I trust you."

A faint pain knifed his heart and was quickly gone. A vision of the past descended on him, grim and mocking, and he could have cursed.

"How can you trust me? You don't know anything at all about me."

"I trust you anyway," she said with simple directness. "Bob trusts you, too. He likes you, Britton. I've just come from him and he told me about you and him and Midnight the other day. He—he said you talked to him like he was a man. He liked that, Britton."

"The kid's all right," Britton said gruffly, staring at the ground. "He just needs a little confidence. He'll find it one of these days."

"Then you'll help him?"

He lifted his eyes and looked at her thoughtfully. He told himself not to have anything to do with her or her brother because there was too much difference between them. Nothing good could ever come of it, only hurt for him. Nevertheless, he said, "I'll do the best I can."

She made a small, pleased sound. "Oh, thank you, Britton," she exclaimed, a little breathlessly. She leaned toward him in earnestness, face turned up to him. "Only don't let Bob ever know I asked it of you. Just kind of ride by now and then and pretend you're visiting with him. He'd be very angry with me if he knew I asked this of you."

"I'll do that," said Britton.

She smiled and started to rein away. A sudden, urgent thought struck him and he told himself instantly not to heed it, but still the words came out of him. "Would you like some coffee? We've got a pot on the fire. It's a long ride back to Chain Link and some coffee would go good." He was not very hopeful that she would accept.

However, she reined the palomino back around and smiled again. "That would be just fine, Britton."

They rode up to the camp site and dismounted. Britton's heart was beating faster. While he was getting a clean cup, he heard Eddie Lane come in. Saddle leather whined as the boy dismounted. Britton got a cup for Lane also.

Lane took off his hat and grinned half bashfully, rolling the brim through his fingers. Stella Hepburn smiled at him and said brightly, "Hello."

"That's Eddie Lane, one of my partners," said Britton.

Lane ducked his head and mumbled, "Pleased to meet you, ma'am."

Britton poured coffee and handed a cup first to the girl. She took a sip and then looked up the canyon at the corrals with a frank interest. "I see you've got a start, Britton," she said.

"We ran those in this morning. That's what's left after we culled them."

"That's a nice start," she said. She turned and stared at him a trifle appraisingly. "Are you a mustanger by trade?"

"No, ma'am. This is my first crack at it." He paused awkwardly, searching for the right way to say things. "I—I'm trying to get a little stake so I can start a ranch of my own." He felt rather embarrassed talking about it. Perhaps it was because it meant so much to him.

"I wish you a lot of luck, Britton," said the girl.

"Thank you, ma'am."

"Company's coming," said Eddie Lane.

Something in the boy's tone pulled Britton around sharply. He saw them then; three riders coming through the mouth of the canyon. One of them was Kyle Reeve and another was Dick Rambone. The third Britton had never seen. He heard the girl suck in her breath and then there was silence, except for the fretful stamping of one of the black's hoofs.

Rambone and his companion rode in ahead of Reeve who had lagged behind. The stranger stared down sternly at the girl. His hair was white at the temples and his mustache was spotted with gray. His eyes were as blue as the girl's, but there the resemblance ended. The man's were hard and glittering.

"So here you are, Stella," he said. "Rambone and I have been looking for you. We hardly expected to find you here."

"I was ready to leave for home, Father," said the girl. She appeared ill at ease. She darted a look at Britton, then quickly averted her eyes. "This is Britton, Father," she went on, "and this is Eddie Lane." Her eyes caught Britton's and held this time. "This is my father, Frank Hepburn."

Hepburn's glance shifted down to Britton and Britton started to nod but Hepburn's eyes just passed on with no acknowledgment. Hepburn turned his head until he was staring up the canyon.

"Take a look, Rambone," he said.

Rambone threw a mocking look at Britton and started his horse. Britton felt anger surge in him as Rambone rode on to the corrals. He was aware that Kyle Reeve had come in and dismounted and was now standing to one side, watching with a faint amusement on his face.

"What's the big idea, Hepburn?" growled Britton.

The look that Hepburn laid on Britton was cold and arrogant. "My foreman's checking the brands on those horses."

"There are no brands on them. Those are mustangs, all of them."

"I'll let my foreman tell me that."

Britton felt blood creep up into his cheeks. He had to clench his fists to contain himself. He was aware of the girl watching him anxiously. He lowered his head and stared darkly at the ground.

Kyle Reeve laughed softly. He had the makin's out and was rolling a cigarette. His head was bowed as he gave his attention to this. "The way the man talks, Steve," Reeve said in an amused tone, "anyone would think you were a jailbird. What's the matter, Hepburn? Can't you see he's got an honest face?"

Britton felt himself go stiff with rage. Don't

ride me, Kyle, he thought with a burst of savagery, damn you, don't you ride me. I know you don't mean anything by it, but don't you ride me . . . The nails were biting into the palms of Britton's hands. Sweat popped out on his brow and clung there in clammy, sticky beads.

Hepburn gave no indication that he had heard. He sat there straight in his saddle, his profile stern and aquiline and unrelenting. His deliberate aloofness was almost like a slap in the face and Britton felt wrath rise in him again but with an effort he swallowed it.

"Get on your horse, Stella," said Frank Hepburn, still staring up the canyon.

The girl threw Britton what was almost an apologetic look. However, she said nothing. Meekly, she went over to the palomino and mounted.

You, too, Stella, Britton was thinking, not only your brother; you're bossed around too. He remembered suddenly how it had been with her and Rambone that other day, how curtly Rambone had ordered her to come and how abjectly she had obeyed. Britton tried to dismiss the thought from his mind, telling himself it was none of his business, but it would not leave.

Rambone returned now. There was insolence in the fleeting look he put on Britton. Rambone's wide mouth held a touch of secret mirth.

"They're all right, Mr. Hepburn, no Chain Link

among them," said Rambone, and then added pointedly, "this time."

Hepburn condescended to lower his glance on Britton. The wind-burned creases of Hepburn's face looked harsh and unbending. "Be sure you keep it like that, Britton."

This time rage burst unchecked in Britton's mind. He made no effort to control it. He lunged ahead a step, glaring up at Hepburn.

"Get off your horses, Hepburn, you and Rambone both," shouted Britton, almost blind with fury. "I've taken all I'm going to take from you. Step down, if both of you ain't yellow."

Resentment and then anger darkened Hepburn's cheeks. Rambone's eyes brightened viciously. Britton jumped ahead and made a grab for Hepburn, intending to pull him out of the saddle, but Lane moved then, grabbing Britton about the waist with both arms.

"Pass it up, Steve," the boy panted, holding tight as Britton strove to break free. "Pass it up."

Rambone jumped his horse ahead, putting it behind Britton and Lane, and the girl cried out in alarm and fright as Rambone started to draw his six-shooter.

Then Kyle Reeve said from the side, very softly, but the tone of it deterred Rambone instantly, "Go right ahead, Rambone. I don't mind busting a few cartridges. Ain't had no excitement in ages anyhow."

Rambone's head turned sharply and his mouth twitched once, spasmodically, when he spied the cocked six-shooter in Reeve's hand. Hepburn too, had laid a hand on his gun, but now he took it away. His face suffused with wrath as he glared down at Britton who had subsided a little.

"Keep what I said in mind, Britton," Hepburn said thinly. "Leave Chain Link stock alone."

Then Hepburn wheeled his horse. "Come, Stella," he snapped, and sent his mount off at a run. The girl cast a white look at Britton. Then Rambone, passing by, slapped the palomino hard on the rump and the horse jumped. The girl made no effort to rein him in. She trailed the two men down the canyon.

Britton stood there, drawing deep breaths. Wrath still roiled in him, he could feel its clawing insistence even in his entrails, his thighs were shuddering from its virulence,

Still watching the three pull away, he said angrily, "How come you rode in with them, Kyle?"

Reeve's brows went up in astonishment. "I wasn't with them, Steve. I ran into them just outside the canyon. They said they were going to check the horses. What did you want me to do? Keep them out?"

Britton said nothing. There was that faint pain in his heart as he thought of the old dream. He went on watching until the three had passed from sight. . . .

4

The next morning the partners rode out again. They had transferred the captured mustangs to another corral and they left the gate of the trap open. They were not too sanguine about finding any horses at the spring, but at midday a small *manada*, herded by a paint, drifted down to the water.

Again Britton waited until the horses had drunk their fill. Then he started the run. Reeve and Lane picked up the band as it emerged from the draw and steered it into the canyon and then into the wing of the trap. This was a small *manada*, only sixteen animals including the stallion. The partners cut out three culls and turned them loose. Then they rode out to check on the barriers around the springs and water holes.

Britton rode northward, almost to the foot of a towering peak. He checked a couple of water holes on the way and found the barriers in place. Then he sent the black on to where Bob Hepburn had his camp.

The boy had put up a rough lean-to at the foot of a bluff. Pines grew all about, shielding the lean-to from the winds which blew off the mountain. Britton found no one there and he was about to ride on when he spied the boy coming in.

The boy smiled shyly when he saw Britton.

"Any luck with Midnight?" asked Britton.

The boy stepped down to the ground. He shook his head. "Got a glimpse of him today, but he was gone before I could do anything about it." He loosened the roan's cinches and the horse drifted over beside the black which was pasturing on the grass.

"You've just got to have patience," said Britton. He had built a cigarette and he was drawing on this. "Horses are smarter than most people give them credit for. Catching Midnight will take some time, but it can be done." He smiled at the boy. "Don't give up, son."

"I won't," said the boy, his lips tightening determinedly. "I knew it wasn't going to be a picnic when I started. I won't quit until I've got him."

"That's the stuff," said Britton.

The boy asked Britton to stay for chow and Britton accepted the invitation. They ate and then they sat around and talked horses. The boy ran off a blue streak and Britton just sat and mostly listened. He appreciated how lonely it must be for the boy with no one to talk to except his sister now and then. Nevertheless, he was making up for it now and it filled Britton with a pleasant glow to see young Hepburn so happy.

It was late when Britton said good night. He

invited the boy to drop in on their camp and then Britton left.

As he turned into the canyon, he saw the flickering of their campfire. He rode directly to a corral and unsaddled the black and turned it into the enclosure. Then he walked to the fire. Eddie Lane was still up. Reeve, however, was rolled in his blankets, back to the fire, making soft sounds as he slept.

In the red glow of the firelight, Lane's face looked grave and anxious. "Where you been, Steve?" he asked. "I was worried something might have happened to you. I was going to ride out and have a look, but Kyle said you'd be all right."

Britton squatted down in front of the fire and spread his hands to warm them. The breeze coming down the canyon was cold. "I ran across young Hepburn and visited with him awhile." When Lane's brows lifted, Britton went on, "He's a nice kid, Eddie. He don't take after his old man at all."

The sound of their voices had wakened Reeve. He rolled over so that he faced them. "You sure it wasn't the Hepburn filly you were visiting with, Steve?" Reeve said with a grin.

Something tightened in Britton's breast. His eyes narrowed. "What makes you say that, Kyle?"

Reeve winked. He was still grinning. "I saw her

look at you, Stevie, boy. Just snap your fingers and she'll come a-running." He chuckled. "Wish she'd look at me that way sometime. I'd know what to do about it."

Something harsh pounded in Britton's heart. "Watch what you say about her, Kyle." His tone was gelid. "I told you that once. Remember it!"

The mirth vanished abruptly from Reeve's features. His mouth started to twitch in the beginning of a snarl. Then he caught himself. His face mirrored the struggle he was putting on to contain himself. When he spoke, his voice was soft, very soft.

"You sure are touchy about her, aren't you?" he said. He rolled over and covered his head with his blankets.

Lane was seated on his bed, pulling off his boots. His glance lay thoughtful and solemn on Britton, but Britton paid him no heed.

Britton straightened slowly and stood there, staring up the canyon, full of the poignancy and hopelessness of his dream. After a while, he stirred and went into the lean-to and got his bedroll. . . .

The partners decided not to run anymore mustangs for several days. They had twenty-nine head in the canyon and they determined to start breaking these.

They took turns topping the wild horses. They

would rope one and drag it into the breaking corral and saddle it. Then one of them would climb aboard and the other two would whip off the blindfold and turn loose their hold and the mustang would go pitching like mad across and around the corral.

It was hard, jarring, teeth-cracking work. There wasn't a one of them that didn't get thrown, and often, even Kyle Reeve who was the best rider of the three. Every time, however, the one who was thrown would get up, cursing and spitting dust, and climb right back on, many times to be thrown all over again.

At sundown they quit. The work of this day had left them spent, too tired even for conversation. They hardly exchanged a word while Britton prepared the inevitable stew and coffee. As soon as they had eaten they crawled into their blankets.

The following day it was the same grueling, dust-churning, body-cracking grind.

They ran into a white-stockinged bay that gave them trouble. He did not look too mean, but once a man got up on top of him the bay turned into the devil incarnate. First, the bay threw Britton twice, quickly, then Lane the same number of times and without much more delay.

Then Reeve tackled the bay. Reeve stuck on a little better, but nevertheless he was thrown three times. The third time he flew from the saddle and landed on his side and slid along in the dust. When he got up, there was a long rent in his sleeve and one cheek was caked with dirt. Reeve grabbed his hat off his head and slammed the Stetson down on the ground. His teeth showed startlingly white against the grime as his face contorted in an irate grimace.

The bay had taken off and run to the far end of the corral. Reeve brandished a fist and cursed it savagely. Then he picked up his hat and slapped at his thighs with it. His whole body was tense with rage as he faced Britton and Lane.

"I've had my fill of this," Reeve snarled, chest heaving, the cords writhing like snakes in his neck. "I've had my fill of working day in and day out without a single, goddam break. I want a woman and I want some whiskey. You might have learned to live like a monk from those years you spent in the pen, Steve, but I haven't. I need a break and I'm taking it. Don't you stand in my way, either. I'm going to Cordova and I'm staying there two-three days until I'm good and ready to come back. You don't like it you know where you can shove it, you and the kid both!"

With that, Reeve stormed out of the corral. His spurs shrilled loudly as he strode to the pen where they kept their saddle mounts. He slapped blanket and saddle and bridle in furious haste on his bay and then he swung up into the kack. The bay kicked up a high string of dust as it pounded at a swift run down the canyon.

Britton sighed wearily and walked out of the corral. Lane followed, a puzzled expression on his face. He turned to look back at the white-stockinged bay prancing nervously and fretfully at the far side of the enclosure. Then Lane shifted his eyes back to Britton; they were still bewildered and worried.

"You think Kyle will be back?" asked the boy.

Britton shrugged. He was rolling a cigarette, trying all the while not to mind a pain in his side where he figured a muscle had been bruised in a fall. "I think so."

"He looked pretty mad."

"Can't say that I blame Kyle," said Britton, and paused to lick the paper. Then he smoothed the cylinder with long, rope-burned fingers. "We could all stand a break."

"You mean you're going into Cordova too?"

"No, nothing like that, Eddie. I'm just knocking off for the rest of the day." He lifted his head and looked at the boy. "You want to go to Cordova? You can if you'd like to."

Lane shook his head. "I'm staying with you, Steve."

Something filled Britton's throat and he was glad of the excuse to duck his head as he lit his cigarette. His eyes had begun to sting. When he looked up again, he found that the boy was watching him closely.

"How can you take all this crap from Kyle?" the boy blurted out.

A muscle bulged along Britton's jaw. "It isn't easy."

"If it wasn't for you, I wouldn't take any of it. You can bet on that," said Lane. His eyes searched Britton's face, seeking something. "How come you threw in with Kyle? You knew all along what he'd be like."

Britton exhaled smoke slowly. "Kyle's all right. He's just a little reckless and lazy. Outside of that he's all right."

"How long have you known him?"

"We were kids together down around Las Cruces."

"You want to tell me anything more, Steve?" Lane's tone was gentle.

Britton glanced sharply at the boy. "I've already told you everything."

"You mean about your prison record?" The boy sounded ill at ease mentioning this. "I'm talking about Kyle. Was he in the pen with you?"

Britton laughed shortly, entirely without mirth. "The only time Kyle ever was in jail was a few Saturday nights when he got too rambunctious. He was always out the next day. He never stayed in for six years."

"Does—does he have anything on you?" Lane sounded very reluctant. Color tinged his cheeks faintly.

Britton peered hard at the boy. "What makes you ask that?"

Lane gestured with a hand. His eyes dropped and he appeared rather uncomfortable. "You keep him on. You go out of your way not to have trouble with him." He stopped and let a silence fall in between them.

Britton drew on his cigarette and exhaled the smoke slowly so that it drifted up in front of his face, veiling his eyes. Through the haze, they looked withdrawn and bitterly reminiscent. After a while, he spoke.

"There's nothing to hold over me. I served my time. I never talk about it because there's nothing to say. I was young and foolish and got in with a bad crowd down around Las Cruces. I thought it was a smart and easy way to make my pile by helping to run wet cattle across the border. Well, I got caught at it."

He paused and drew again on his smoke. The hollows seemed deeper than ever in his cheeks, not even the black beard stubble could conceal that. His lids were narrowed in galling recollection.

"I was young," he went on, "but I won't say I didn't know what I was doing. I just thought I was being smart. Well, six years in the pen changed my way of thinking. Mind you, I'm not saying the punishment changed it. When a man's really set on something, neither punishment nor kindness can change him. I just came to realize that stealing wasn't right. Taking other people's property just isn't right. I'll never steal again, anything, not because I'm afraid of being caught and punished, but because it just isn't right."

Britton took another drag on his cigarette and then he dropped the butt and ground it out under a heel. He was awhile like that, staring morosely down. In his heart that faint pain and the hopelessness were echoing again. It seemed they would stay around awhile this time.

"What was Kyle like in those days?" the boy asked, when Britton showed he was not going to continue.

"Kyle was no better than me. The only difference was that he didn't get caught."

"How come you threw in with him then? Especially since you're going straight?"

Britton's head came up. A small, bitter smile lifted one corner of his mouth briefly. "I'm an ex-con. Who could I get to throw in with me? Who could I get to trust me? You took me at my word that I was going straight, but how many others would have?"

The boy kicked at the ground in embarrassment. He said nothing.

Britton turned and looked at the white-stockinged bay which was starting to prance restlessly around the corral. "Let's get that rig off that bronc," he said, "and then we'll call it a day. . . ."

· · ·

When they had unsaddled the mustang, they returned to their camp site. Britton started a fire and put the coffeepot on. Then he put some water on to heat. Somehow, the idea of knocking off made him feel restful, the edge was gone from everything. He figured Reeve had been right. They'd been driving themselves too hard. A day or two more on the job did not mean much against the spread of a lifetime.

When the water was warm, Britton dug out his mirror and razor and soap and then he shaved. Looking at himself in the glass afterward, he saw that his skin had started to pale where the whiskers had concealed it. His mouth seemed a little tighter and sterner and his cheeks a trifle gaunter. The skin stretched very tautly over the high bones under his eyes.

He poured two cups of coffee and carried them over to Eddie Lane who was sitting on a rock, strumming his guitar and humming softly. The boy took a sip of coffee and said, "Man, this tastes good."

Britton grinned. Somehow he felt elated, just him and the boy here and nothing to do the rest of the day. "Is that what you're really thinking about this coffee?"

The boy laughed, a loud, merry sound. "Do you really want to know what I think?"

"Let's stay friends," said Britton. He grinned again.

The boy chuckled. He struck several more chords on the guitar, soft, sad, lingering sounds. His face grew pensive. The focus of his eyes drifted far away.

"I wonder what Mona's doing," he said, his voice tender. His eyes stayed away. A small, wan smile took over his mouth. "You know, I miss her very much, Steve."

Britton said nothing. He sat down on the ground with his back against the rock and sipped his coffee. He was thinking of a woman, too, but there was little joy in his thoughts, only futility and hurt. Above him, Lane struck another chord and the strings hummed awhile as though reluctant to let go of the sound.

"She's seventeen," Lane said after a while. "Did I ever tell you that, Steve? Maybe she's too young. Maybe I'm too young. Still, we're pretty sure we're in love. She's never had no one else. It's been the same with me. There will never be anyone for me except Mona."

Lane paused and the guitar sounded again. "We've got a house all picked out in Palo Pinto. It's an old house and run down, but me and Mona figure we can fix it up good. Some paint outside and inside will make it look like new. Mona figures on putting bright curtains in the windows and making rag rugs for the floors. It's a wonder what Mona can do with a needle and thread, even though she's just seventeen."

Britton sat and listened. He said nothing. His throat was too full for him to speak even if he'd been of a mind to.

The boy strummed another chord. This was a sharp, happy one. "Why don't you come visit us sometime, Steve? Wouldn't that be nice? I know Mona would be very glad to have you. I know she'd like you and I'm sure you'll like Mona. You could even come to live with us if you don't have anywhere else to go. Mona wouldn't mind. But then, you'll probably be getting married someday, too. Say," he cried, as if a sudden thought had struck him; "when you get married we could settle down next to each other and visit back and forth. Wouldn't that be nice, Steve?"

"Sure," said Britton, his eyes on the far distances, pain in the walls of his throat. "That would be very nice, Eddie."

"Just think of it," murmured the boy, "you and your wife and me and my Mona living next to each other. I don't think I'd like anything better than that." He struck another chord and then began to sing.

"Down in the valley,
The valley so low,
Hang your head over,
Hear the wind blow . . ."

Britton took another sip of coffee and narrowed his eyes as he thought. A vision of Stella Hepburn drifted in front of him and with it came the feeling of utter uselessness. He began to get angry.

"If you don't love me,
Love whom you please;
Throw your arms round me,
Give my heart ease . . ."

Why couldn't it be? Britton began to think, anger running through him. He had paid all the debt he owed to anyone. He had more than paid. Why should a thing like that be held against a man? Shouldn't it be laid away and forgotten, provided the man had paid and changed?

"Throw your arms round me
Before it's too late;
Throw your arms round me,
Feel my heart break . . ."

Britton twirled the cup in his fingers and his mind wandered to a world far away. It was the world of his dream, the dream born of shame and repentance and bitter loneliness and pain of heart. When he was in this world, he forgot everything. Everything, it seemed, except that pain. That part of it somehow never left him.

"Roses love sunshine,
Violets love dew;
Angels in heaven
Know I love you . . ."

The next morning they were up at dawn. After a hurried breakfast, they went up to the corrals. The sky was yellow in the east. The tops of the mountains were clear and distinct in the light of the rising sun, but patches of shadow still clung to the lower slopes and canyons.

Britton roped a mustang and dragged it into the breaking corral. They had to throw it and blindfold it in order to get the saddle and hackamore on. They loosed the horse's legs and the animal came upright, standing there all atremble with uncertainty and fear. Lane climbed aboard. When he gave the signal, Britton whipped off the blindfold and the mustang went bucking across the corral.

Another day's work had begun.

They knocked off for dinner which consisted of black coffee and jerky and dried apples. Then they smoked a couple of cigarettes and returned to the horses.

The dun threw Britton and when he came to his feet he saw that Lane was watching something coming up the canyon. Turning his glance that way, Britton spied the two riders. He went over and stood beside the boy. The dun was still pitching about the corral, but they paid it no heed.

"Is that Kyle?" asked Lane.

Britton squinted awhile and then his heart gave a sudden turn. "No, that's not Kyle," he said. He stood there, watching the riders come on. Soon they were close enough for Lane to recognize them also.

The riders were Bob and Stella Hepburn.

They reined in and dismounted. Britton stepped outside the corral to greet them. Lane followed. Young Hepburn showed Britton that shy smile.

"I tracked Midnight to that spring you've left open," said Hepburn, "but he got away from me. Then Stella showed up and we thought we'd drop in on you and say hello."

Britton introduced Hepburn to Lane. The two youths shook hands. Hepburn's eyes were bright and eager on the dun in the corral.

"You breaking him?" he asked Lane.

"Yeah. He just threw Steve."

"Mind if I give him a whirl?" Hepburn asked, turning to Britton.

"Go right ahead," said Britton.

Stella Hepburn made a slight, protesting sound that only Britton heard. Hepburn was already going into the corral. Britton smiled reassuringly at the girl.

"He'll be all right."

Lane roped the dun and blindfolded it. Hepburn

stepped up into the saddle, settled himself and signaled Lane. Lane whipped off the blindfold and the dun whirled around completely once and then started crow hopping.

The girl watched with her face a trifle pale. Britton stared at her, conscious of the quickened rate of his heart and of the thickness in his throat. She cried out when Hepburn lost his seat and slid out of the saddle. But he bounded to his feet, shouting for another try. Lane started after the dun with his rope.

"The kid rides good," Britton said quietly. "He'd make a hand anywhere. I'd give odds he rides the dun this time."

Britton was right. Hepburn stuck in the saddle like a burr and after a while the dun straightened out and ran around the corral once and then slowed down and stopped, flanks heaving and head hanging in an admission of defeat.

Hepburn came out of the corral with his face aglow. "Did you see me, Stella?" he cried exuberantly. "Broke him slick as a whistle. I'm gonna do the same to Midnight. You just watch and see."

Britton glanced at the sun and saw that it was late afternoon. He felt weary and worn after having been at it since sunrise, so he told Lane to unsaddle the dun and they'd call it a day. Hepburn went to help Lane and the girl walked with Britton back to the camp site.

Britton started the fire and put on the coffee. He straightened to find the girl staring gravely and thoughtfully at him. She did not glance away when he met her eyes, although a bit of color tinted her cheeks.

"Looks like you've got a start on that ranch, Britton," she said.

"That's right."

Her eyes appeared to be searching for something in his face. Of course, he had shaved yesterday, he thought. Without the whiskers he looked different. Perhaps that was why she stared at him in such a manner.

"Are you going to live on that ranch alone, Britton?"

His heart turned sad. "I suppose so."

"Don't you have anyone? A—a family?"

"My family's been dead since I was fourteen."

"It's not much fun living alone, is it?"

He stared at her solemnly. Color rose in her face, but she did not look away. "No, it isn't," he said. Then a sudden boldness possessed him. "Maybe I'll do something about it—after I've got that ranch." His throat went dry.

Her glance still did not waver. "I think you should," she said, barely above a whisper.

Something overwhelming seized him. He would tell her, he decided. He would end the agonizing suspense once and for all. He would tell her what he was and what he had been and then it would be up to her. If she chose not to come around anymore, he would have to begin to forget, which, sad as it might be, would be better than eating his heart out over a dream that had no chance.

He had just opened his mouth when the sound of spurs angled in, halting him before he had uttered a single word. Lane and Hepburn came walking in and Britton knew the moment was gone. How-ever, another time would come. He promised himself that.

The two youths were busy talking horses. They seemed hardly aware of Britton and the girl, but the spell was broken. When the coffee was ready, Britton handed her a cup and stood beside her. They drank without exchanging a word.

Then Hepburn went and got the palomino and his roan. He and his sister mounted. She hesitated an instant, staring with that same gravity down at Britton, and he thought he read some-thing for him alone in her eyes, and this both elated and saddened him. Then she turned the palomino and lifted it into a trot.

She twisted in the saddle once and waved an arm in farewell. Britton returned the gesture. After that, he stood and watched, and listened to the hard, measured beating of his heart. . . .

The paint threw Lane for the third time and the boy jumped to his feet, cursing savagely. His hat had come off and he walked over and picked it up, still swearing. He slapped some of the dust off his thighs and then jammed the Stetson on his head. He was still cursing.

Britton got his rope and went after the paint. He cornered it and dropped a loop over its head and got the blindfold on after a struggle. Lane was swearing yet.

"When the hell is that goddam Kyle coming back?" cried the boy, face flushed with wrath. The cords stood out like cables in his neck. "Four days he's been gone. I wouldn't say anything if it was two or even three, but he's overdoing it. When the hell's he coming back from Cordova?"

"Maybe he isn't coming back," said Britton.

"He'll be back all right," snarled the boy. "You just watch and see. He'll wait until he figures we've got these broncs busted and then he'll show up. He ain't running out on us anymore, not when there's money involved. He'll be right on hand pronto when we sell the broncs and get ready to split the dinero. He won't be late then."

Britton swung up on the paint, feeling it gather and tense under him like a coiled spring ready to let loose. He waited until Lane came over and whipped off the blindfold. The paint took off in a straight line, stiff-legged hops jarring Britton from the end of the spine to the top of his skull.

The paint slammed up against the wall of the corral, intending to scrape Britton out of the kack, but he had seen it coming and he swung his leg out of the way, for a moment staying on with only one foot in a stirrup. As the paint whirled away, snorting angrily, Britton settled back in the saddle and found the other stirrup again.

The paint reared high, thrashing the air with its forelegs. An instant it wavered there as though it were going to crash down on its back. Britton slapped it on top of the skull with the end of the hackamore rope and the paint dropped down on its four feet. It kicked up its rear end once and then took off at a whirling, weaving run. It made one turn around the corral like this, then it straightened out and Britton reined it down to a trot and then pulled it in.

The paint was broken.

Britton stepped down to the ground with sweat streaming down his cheeks. He loosened the cinches and pulled the saddle off the now docile paint. Lane led it into the adjoining corral and slipped off the hackamore.

The sun was just above the mountain peaks in the west. Britton gave it a glance and said, "That's enough for today."

He and Lane started for the camp site, their dragging boots drawing tired funnels in the sand. Britton had just started arranging the firewood when he heard Lane say wryly:

"Well, well, if it ain't the prodigal son returning."

Straightening, Britton threw a look down the canyon. An uneasy prescience settled over him when he saw that there were two riders. He could not explain why he felt this way.

"Now who the hell is that with him?" asked Lane.

Britton glanced at the irate boy. "Take it easy, Eddie," he said quietly. "We won't gain anything by quarreling with Kyle. Take it easy, won't you?"

The boy's lips tightened. A dark look suffused his face. "All right," he muttered. "I'll let it ride for now. But when this is all over, Kyle is going to hear from me. You won't stop me then, Steve."

Lane was peering intently as the riders drew closer. The boy swore. "I'll be damned. That's a woman with him, Steve."

She was wearing men's clothing, a red plaid shirt and faded blue Levi's. Her hat dangled down her back from the chin thongs about her neck. Her hair was dark and cropped short, lending a boyish cast to her round face.

Reeve waved a hand in greeting and grinned as he reined in his bay and dismounted. The girl stepped down from her pinto, the Levi's stretching tight over her hips as she did so, and Reeve slapped her playfully there. She turned her head and threw him a grin over her shoulder.

"This is Carmen, boys," said Reeve, hitching

up his chaps. With a languid hand, he pointed out his partners. "Carmen, this is Steve Britton and Eddie Lane." Reeve winked at Britton and grinned. "Carmen's gonna stay with us and take over the cooking. I can't stand your stew no more, Stevie boy, but Carmen's gonna fix that. Aren't you, honey?"

The girl smiled. She had small, even teeth and a long dimple in each cheek. "Hello, Steve," she said. "Hello, Eddie." Her voice was low and throaty.

The wrath had disappeared from Lane. He took off his hat and nodded bashfully.

Britton said nothing. His face turned stern. A vicious resentment started building up in him and he had to exert all his will to keep himself in hand. The girl must have sensed some of this for her smile flickered and then went out. A worried shadow crossed her face.

"Come, Carmen," said Reeve. "I'll show you where the things are."

He indicated the cooking utensils and then he got down on his knees and started the fire. It was the first time Britton had seen Reeve light anything except a cigarette.

There was a roll behind the girl's saddle and Lane untied this and placed it on the ground. Then he led the pinto and the bay toward the corrals. Britton went over to a rock and sat down. Taking out the makin's, he built a cigarette and sat there smoking, a scowl on his face as he watched Reeve and the girl.

Reeve hovered very close to her as if his help were indispensable to the preparation of the meal. He kept whispering things to her and every now and then she would giggle. Once she laughed, a happy, intimate sound, and something touched Britton's heart. Immediately after, however, the rage came.

He stood up so abruptly that his spurs sounded faintly. He pinched out his smoke and flung it to the ground. In the gathering dusk his face looked hard and implacable.

"Kyle," he said, his voice thick with the restraint he imposed on it. "Come here."

Without waiting to see if Reeve was going to respond, Britton turned and walked off. Behind him, he could hear the singing of Reeve's spurs as the man followed. Britton halted and came around, the fingers of his right hand drumming impatiently against his thigh as he waited for Reeve to come up.

Reeve looked jaunty as he approached. His Stetson was cocked on one side of his head and under the tawny mustache his mouth held the trace of a smile. He came to a stop and touched his silky sideburns while his glance probed at the expression on Britton's face. What Reeve saw there disturbed him not a bit. The smile widened his mouth a trifle more.

"Yes, Steve?" he said softly, unctuously. His tone carried a shadow of amusement.

"Get her out of here," Britton said with low, quivering fury. "Send her packing quick."

One brow of Reeve's lifted. His smile widened. "Why would I want to do a thing like that? She won't get in anybody's way. She'll cook and help out around the camp." Sarcasm entered his tone. "You can deduct the grub she eats from my share."

"Damn the grub she eats," snarled Britton. "Get rid of her!"

Reeve lifted a hand and brushed his mustache. A speculative glitter brightened his eyes. He was awhile like that, searching Britton's face as though trying to read his innermost thoughts.

"Carmen stays," Reeve said quietly. "Maybe I should have told you right off. I married the girl."

On the instant, Britton was stunned. Reeve noticed his partner's consternation and laughed softly.

"Yes, sir, Stevie boy," Reeve said. "I can't believe it myself yet. It used to be love 'em and leave 'em for me, but those days are gone. It's only Carmen for me from now on."

Britton still could not speak. Something vaguely troubling and ominous was picking away at his mind and what made it so exasperating was that he could not define it. He knew only that he did not like it.

Reeve frowned as though puzzled by Britton's silence. "Don't you believe me, Steve? There's a padre in Cordova and he tied the knot tight and legal. I've got the license, case you want to see it."

Britton drew a deep breath. A hush of sadness and poignancy gripped him briefly. In this moment, he had a vision of a blond-haired girl. Then it passed and left his loneliness and hopelessness more pronounced than ever.

"She's gonna bring us trouble, Kyle," he said quietly. "We've got enough of it on our hands without bringing her into it."

"What trouble could she bring? I married her, didn't I? Nobody's gonna come looking for her."

"I just don't like having a woman in camp. Send her back to Cordova."

Reeve cocked his head to one side. His right hand lifted and pulled pensively at his sideburns. In the thickening shadows his features looked withdrawn. It was as though he were meditating on something profound.

After a while, he said, steel in his tone, "As long as I stay, she stays, Steve. Get that through your head." When Britton opened his mouth to speak, Reeve held up a hand, deterring him. "I had the idea from the beginning that we were partners. However, you started bossing us right from the start. Maybe because I took it you've become bossier right along. Well, I'm telling you you're through bossing me. If the kid wants to take orders from you, that's his business, but you're through telling *me* what to do. Understand? If anyone's moving out of this camp, Steve, it's gonna be you and not me or Carmen. Is that clear?"

"I'm not trying to boss anybody," Britton said through his teeth. "I'm just trying to tell you what's best. I've got nothing against the girl. I just don't want trouble. We've got enough of it with Chain Link snooping around as though we were stealing their horses and cattle."

"Don't blame me for that," Reeve said with a sneer. "I'm not the ex-con of this outfit."

This time the wrath burst unchecked in Britton. He made no attempt to hold himself in. Stepping ahead swiftly, he grabbed the front of Reeve's shirt before the man could react and fall back. A hard jerk yanked Reeve up on his toes.

"Listen to me, Kyle," snarled Britton, his face just inches from Reeve's. Fury spasmed and stormed in Britton, its virulence set him to trembling. "Don't you ride me about being in the pen. Don't you ever ride me about that again. This is the last time I'm telling you."

Reeve's hand rose and closed hard about Britton's wrist, but he would not let go. Reeve's teeth showed white in a grimace of wrath and hate.

"All right," he growled, "but Carmen stays."

"Don't let her bring trouble then," said Britton.

"If she does, I'll have it out with you. I'll have it out if it's the last thing I do."

With that, Britton released his grip and gave a shove that sent Reeve back a couple of steps. His spurs caught in the ground and he stumbled and almost fell, but he recovered in time and stood there, glowering at Britton. Slowly, automatically, Reeve stuffed his shirt back inside his trousers and then hitched up his belt. All the while his irate gaze never left Britton.

"Next time you lay a hand on me, Steve," Reeve said in a peculiar, deadly voice, "you'd better be prepared for something. I don't like people pawing me or pushing me around. Have you got that?"

He glared at Britton a moment longer. Then Reeve wheeled and strode off, his spurs shrieking. He did not stop until he reached the fire. He halted there and stared down at the flames awhile. Then suddenly, viciously, he kicked at a brand and a shower of sparks shot up.

Britton stood where he was, waiting for the rage to die in him. He was still quivering from its ravages. Something insufferable seemed to be balled in his chest and he was waiting for it to dissipate.

Eventually, the fury passed. Now he felt weak and tired and disgusted. He took out the makin's, scarcely knowing that he was doing so, and when he had them in his hands he found he did not want a smoke, so he returned them to his pocket.

He drew a deep breath and started ahead. Lane had returned from caring for the horses and he stood to one side, watching Britton walk in. The boy's attitude indicated that he was aware of what had passed between Britton and Reeve. Lane's glance was frankly inquiring as it rested on Britton, but Britton said nothing. He went over and sat down on a rock at the edge of the firelight.

The girl was busy with the cooking. Nevertheless, she threw a look over her shoulder once at Britton. When she saw him sitting there, sullen and brooding, his dark face sinistrous in the shadows, she quickly brought her head back. After that, she kept her attention fixed almost forcibly on what she was doing.

Reeve had gone over and sat down on the pile of firewood. The tip of his cigarette glowed red every time he drew on it. Lane had taken his bedroll out of the lean-to and he was seated on his blankets. No one spoke. The only sounds were the cracking of pine knots and the occasional clatter of a pan.

Finally, the girl went and got the plates. She filled the first one and carried it over to Britton. Something sullen and resentful stirred in him as he watched her come. She had fried steak and potatoes and she also had a cup of coffee. She extended these to Britton, the tentative beginning of a smile on her mouth.

Then she saw the darkness and the thin-lipped animosity on his face and the smile died before it was born. A look that verged on fear crossed her face and she turned and went quickly back to the fire.

Britton ate glumly. His baleful glance followed the girl as she served Lane and then Reeve. She helped herself last of all and then she went and sat down next to Reeve.

Britton sat on his rock, alone and bitter, hardly aware of what the food tasted like. He tried thinking of the dream but tonight, strangely, it would not come. All that his mind would hold were dark, brooding thoughts and a premonition of evil. This last sensation was quite sharp and distinct. . . .

5

Britton awoke with the smell of boiling coffee in his nose. Sitting up in his blankets, he saw the girl seated by the fire, mixing something in a pan. Britton pulled on his boots and stood up. The girl threw him a look, but he pretended not to have seen it. He started for the spring, his spurs jingling softly in the early dawn.

Britton washed up and when he returned he saw that Lane was awake, rubbing his eyes and yawning. The girl smiled at Lane and said good morning and he smiled in return. He stopped to exchange a few words with her before continuing on to the spring.

Britton stood to one side and rolled a cigarette. He was aware all the while that the girl kept throwing glances at him, but he kept his head bowed, giving her not the slightest heed. He lighted the cigarette and then heard the girl say:

"Coffee's ready if you want some, Steve."

The low, rich timbre of her voice somehow kindled a feeling of loneliness in him. He could not understand why it should do this and it made him angry.

Almost grudgingly, he approached the fire. She had already filled a cup and she held this up to him. He took it, his eyes locking with hers. She tried to hold the gaze but, after a while, the sternness of his made her shift her eyes.

He stood there, staring down at her. With her head bowed, he could see the fine lines of her profile. She was quite pretty with her deeply tanned skin and rich lips and long-lashed dark eyes. There was a tiny scar on one cheek and, strangely enough, this enhanced rather than detracted from her looks.

Lane returned from the spring and at the same time Reeve emerged from the lean-to where he had slept. The girl's head came up and she called Reeve's name happily. He grinned and came swaggering over to her, yawning and scratching his sides.

Britton drifted over to a rock and sat down and sipped his coffee. He was aware of Eddie Lane watching him thoughtfully all the while.

They had flapjacks and syrup, which Reeve must have brought back from Cordova for Britton could not recall having purchased any when he had laid in their supplies. There were also fried bacon and eggs, other items Reeve must have picked up. Britton could not recall the last time he had eaten as well. Nevertheless, he felt dis-gruntled and restless.

When he was through eating, Britton started for the corrals without a word to his partners. Lane followed soon after and came up as Britton was saddling his black. The boy looked ill at ease and patently worried.

"Where to today, Steve?" he asked.

Britton shrugged. He did not feel like talking, but then he told himself the boy was not responsible for his mood. It was strictly between him and Reeve.

"I'm scouting around. Maybe I'll pick up some new mustang sign."

"Want me to do the same?"

"Suit yourself."

"Ah, Steve," said the boy. He sounded hurt.

Sudden contrition struck Britton. He turned and laid a hand on Lane's arm. "I'm sorry, Eddie," he said. "You scout around, too. It's time we picked up some more horses."

"What about Kyle?"

Britton swung up on the black. He fitted his toes carefully in the stirrups and then he leaned forward in the saddle and looked down at the boy. The corners of Britton's mouth were pulled in, the short beard stubble seemed to bristle as the line of his jaw hardened.

"I don't give a damn what Kyle does. He can sit around on his thumbs all day long for all I care."

He saw the boy's face slack with surprise and hurt, but the rage was suddenly so great in Britton that he did not care. He started the black and rode down the canyon. As he passed the camp site, he was conscious of Reeve and the girl watching him, but Britton kept his eyes straight ahead.

In him, that premonition of disaster seemed stronger than ever. Not even the dream could ease the feeling this morning, it seemed. . . .

When he saw the smoke, Britton reined in. It was only a thin wisp, barely visible, and he had to squint his eyes to make sure it was not an illusion. A vague uneasiness settled over him, but he could not explain it.

As far as Britton knew, there was no one living in this part of the Ladrones. The land was too isolated and harsh to tempt anyone into taking up permanent residence. The ranching country lay beyond, where Chain Link began. He thought of young Hepburn, but the boy's camp was not here, unless he had moved it.

Britton started the black and rode on. The smoke disappeared as though someone had doused the fire. The black moved down a grade and passed through some junipers. When it emerged on the other side of the trees, Britton saw where the fire had been.

He halted the black and studied the spot, that feeling of uncomfortableness tickling his spine again. Only charred sticks and ashes remained and they were scattered as though someone had kicked the fire apart. One stick still emitted a tiny curl of smoke.

That sensation of portent grew stronger than ever in Britton and suddenly he realized that it was no longer a feeling but a reality. His head came up sharply, breath catching for an instant in his throat, and he saw the riders, three of them, sitting their horses on a rise a short distance away.

They were watching Britton. He edged the black around until he was facing them squarely. They went on watching awhile longer. Then, in unison, they started their horses and came riding in on him.

Britton waited. His heart had quickened, he could hear the sound of its beating. The black pricked up its ears and whinnied softly and one of the horses replied.

The riders pulled up in front of Britton. They nodded to him and he returned the gesture. Their glances rested on him, cool, wary and slyly appraising. That sensation of uneasiness traveled down Britton's spine again.

One of the riders began searching in the pockets of his vest and shirt. He was a tall, thin fellow with the skin drawn very tightly over the sharp angles of his face. His pale blue eyes had a wide, direct, unwinking stare like that of the dead. His hands were long-fingered with large, prominent knuckles. After several moments of searching, he came up with an empty Bull Durham sack.

"Got any spare tobacco, friend?" he asked Britton. "I seem to be fresh out."

Britton took out the makin's and handed them over. The thin man rolled a cigarette and then passed the sack on to his companions. When they had rolled themselves smokes, the thin man returned the sack to Britton.

"Thanks, friend," the thin man said.

Britton did not speak. He sat there on the black, disturbed by something he could not comprehend. He had never seen these three before, yet they were regarding him with a crafty, deliberate curiosity. Britton could not shake the feeling that it was more than a passing interest.

The thin man exhaled smoke and said, "You a rider for one of the local outfits?"

Britton shook his head. "I'm on my own."

A flicker of interest showed briefly in the wide, glassy stare. "You have your own spread then?"

"I'm mustanging."

"Oh?" the thin man said. He shifted slightly in the saddle and took another drag on his smoke. "We've seen quite a few mustangs here in the Ladrones. Looks like you've picked a good spot, partner. Having any luck?"

"Tolerable," said Britton.

The thin man inhaled on his cigarette and held the smoke in his mouth awhile. His face looked as though his thoughts were far away. At last, he blew the smoke out slowly. It drifted up, veiling his eyes.

"I'm called Mingo," the thin man said. He waved a hand, indicating his partners. "That's Ben Surratt and this is Randy Gerber."

"I'm Britton."

Surratt and Gerber nodded again by way of acknowledging the introduction. Surratt was a middle-aged man with an ample paunch and pink jowls that flowed over the buttoned collar of his shirt. His face held a bland expression that was too studied to be natural.

Gerber looked like he was in his early twenties. He was blond and he was trying to raise a mustache, but it was so pale that it hardly stood out. He had small, bright eyes that twinkled with no trace whatever of mirth.

There was something about the three that troubled Britton, something that he felt he should know, but he could not put his finger on it. This failure left him feeling disgusted and uneasy.

"Well, thanks for the tobacco, friend," said Mingo. He lifted a hand in a brief gesture of farewell and turned his horse. He rode off with his companions following.

Britton watched until they were over the rise and it was not until then that it dawned on him what had been so strange about the three. They had never once looked at the remnants of the dead fire. It was as if they had known all the time it was there. . . .

• • •

The next morning Britton rode out again as soon as he had eaten. He went to young Hepburn's camp and had a short visit with the boy and then rode on. Around noon, he spotted a large band of mustangs in a canyon and he paused to make a careful survey of the site.

He did not work in too close because he did not want to startle and stampede the horses. Sticking to the timbered slopes of the canyon, he made his way around the band without the mustangs becoming aware of him. He sent the black on to see if the canyon had a box end, but it did not, so Britton rode back.

The mustangs still grazed on the canyon floor. Several of them spotted him as he passed through a break in the trees and they threw up their heads and snorted, but they did not run. He left them as they were and rode out of the canyon.

He headed for the nearest water hole that had been fenced off and while he was still some distance away he saw that the barrier was down. At first, he assumed it had been the work of mustangs, but when he drew nearer he saw that the job was too thorough for an animal. It was human hands and intelligence that had done this.

A bitter wrath rose in Britton. He dismounted and rebuilt the barrier. All around the water hole he saw tracks where mustangs had come in to drink. These tracks had also obliterated any sign of whoever had broken the fence. Nevertheless, Britton had an idea and he was pretty sure he was correct. Briefly, a feeling of futility swept over him because it seemed everything was going wrong and bad. Nothing was working out right anymore.

When he was done, Britton mounted the black and rode on, raging quietly inside. He tried the dream to see if that would still the turmoil within him, but the dream only sputtered and then would not come anymore. He tried thinking of Stella Hepburn, but today everything kept telling him he had no chance there and thoughts of her faded too. A picture of Carmen came once, startlingly bright across his mind, and he dismissed it almost viciously.

Then all at once he picked up the tracks of a single horseman and every other consideration fled Britton's mind. A vile eagerness possessed him as he sent the black in pursuit. He realized that the tracks could very well have been laid down by either Lane or Reeve, but there was one other possibility and it filled Britton with a cruel anticipation. He could be wrong, but if he wasn't—

The tracks cut across a plain and then snaked up the side of a rock-strewn ridge, heading in the direction of the next water hole. Britton urged the black on to a lope and when he topped the ridge he spotted the rider below.

Exultation and then wrath, primal and ugly and brutal, filled Britton's breast. His eyes slitted and his lips pulled back an instant from his teeth in a silent snarl. Everything else was forgotten except the rider below. Without being aware of doing so, Britton's right hand loosened the .44 in its holster. Then he was sending the black down the slope at a swift run.

The rider heard the sounds behind him and he hipped around, startled, in the kack and when he saw it was Britton, the horseman wheeled his mount quickly to face him. The rider was Dick Rambone.

Britton reined in the black and sat in the saddle, staring at Rambone. If Rambone had experienced any astonishment, he had had time to mask his feelings. His dark features were as bland and quietly insolent as ever. Only a slight narrowing of his eyes betrayed an inner wariness.

Britton did not say anything. He could not trust himself to speak and then he wanted Rambone to start it.

After a long while, Rambone stirred slightly and folded his wrists over the saddle horn. He peered at Britton a moment more, arrogance pulling down the corners of his mouth, and then Rambone said:

"Howdy, Britton."

By now Britton felt he had himself sufficiently in hand. His heart still pounded with hard, stinging strokes, but the unreasoning frenzy was gone from his brain.

"What're you doing here?" he growled.

Rambone's brows went up as though he were going to take umbrage at Britton's question. Then the Chain Link ramrod's eyes frosted over and became empty of any noticeable expression.

"Looking for strays," he said in that deep, quiet way of his.

"Is that all?"

Rambone considered this a moment, his face blank. His eyes appeared to be looking right through Britton. Then Rambone said, "What else would there be?" He was giving the impression that he was weighing every word deliberately.

"Is it Chain Link's custom," said Britton, fighting to keep his tone calm, "to send the foreman out after strays? What do the other hands do?"

Rambone looked down at his wrists still crossed on the horn and smiled faintly. "Whatever I tell them to."

"Why did you pull that fence down around that water hole?"

This brought Rambone's head up. Britton's tone had been sharp, but he felt it was more than this that had alerted Rambone. The man seemed to draw back warily in the saddle. His eyes brightened.

"What're you talking about?"

"You know what. You pulled that fence down."

"Did you see me, Britton?"

"I didn't have to see you. If you say you didn't do it, you're a goddam liar!"

Rambone tensed. Slowly, he took his wrists off the horn. He came up very straight in the saddle and his hands moved carefully back, the right one coming to a stop just below the tip of his holster. The blandness was gone from Rambone's face. It looked taut and mean.

"For a greasy-sack mustanger," Rambone said, and his tone was heavy with contempt and insolence, "you're mighty free and easy with your words. Has it ever occurred to you that you might have to back them up?"

Rage was hammering behind Britton's eyes. The portent of what might lie ahead was very apparent to him, but he did not care, even though it might involve his own death. He had finally reached a point of insufferableness and he could endure it no longer.

He reined the black a little to the side to give him more room. Britton's hand came to a rest beside his holstered .44. Heedlessness was running through him like a strong current.

"I'm not afraid to back them up, if that's what you mean," Britton said coldly. "Make your play, Rambone."

For an instant, Rambone's eyes glowed brightly

as if triumph had entered them. One corner of his wide mouth lifted in a tiny, gloating smirk. Then his features were abruptly gelid and cruel, and it came to Britton that the time for it was at hand.

Britton knew nothing except the realization that within a minute he might be dead, but still this did not frighten or deter him. He figured death was better than the constant thwarting of everything he aspired to. So he tensed and waited for Rambone to draw his gun.

Then the sound came. Rambone heard it the same instant Britton did. Rambone's chin tilted ever so slightly and though his eyes were still riveted on Britton it became apparent that Rambone was dividing his attention, straining to hear more of the sound that was coming up behind him.

Britton had only to avert his glance a little and he saw it. The pinto approached at a walk. The sound came again as one of its shod hoofs struck a stone. Carmen sat very still in the saddle. It was obvious that she understood what was under way.

Nevertheless, she came on and rode the pinto in between Rambone and Britton and halted it there. She turned her face toward Britton and he read the bright fear but also the resolution in the dark eyes. The color had faded from her lips and they looked dry and tight, but she stayed there in the line of fire between the two men.

Rambone appeared to have frozen in the saddle. For several moments he did not move, not even his chest rose to indicate that he was breathing. His unwinking eyes grew brighter than ever and a deep thoughtfulness lay in the cast of his countenance. Then he loosened up. His breath made a soft, audible sound as he let it out. His eyes grew veiled and the old insolence returned

to the shape of his mouth. His right hand rose slowly and carefully and closed about the saddle horn.

"We'll meet again, Britton," Rambone said quietly. He spurred his horse and went off at a hard run.

Britton watched until Rambone was out of sight. Gradually, the tension eased in Britton. Reaction came now, fluttering the muscles of his thighs and putting a momentary weakness in his belly as he thought how rash he had been and how small a thing this was to have died for.

He turned his head to look at the girl and saw that she had reined the pinto away a little. Her head was bowed and her profile was to him and for a moment the thought came to Britton that she looked like a repentant child caught in some mischief. This feeling was fleeting, however, for then the resentment came.

"You know you might have been killed, don't you?" he growled.

She kept her head down and did not face him. Her voice was small. "I didn't know how else to stop it."

"You didn't *have* to stop it."

"He might have killed you, Steve." Her lips moved very stiffly. "He looks like he's good with a gun."

"Maybe I'm good with one too."

"And maybe you aren't. Is death worth risking to find out?" Her head had come up and there was a measure of defiance in her voice.

He found he could not answer this. He went on staring at her. The sun was very bright on her face and he could see the tiny scar on her cheek and the squint wrinkles at the edges of her eyes. She was quite young, he thought, around nineteen or so, and she looked very pretty even with the revealing harshness of the sun on her. Then he caught himself and grew angry with this way of thinking. He did not like her, he reminded him-self. He would never like her because in the short while she had been in camp the old dream had grown halfhearted and faint.

"What're you doing away from camp?" he growled.

"I got tired of staying there." She faced him now and her chin lifted as if in a challenge. "I was all alone and so I thought I'd ride around a bit. Maybe I can find mustang sign, too, even though I'm just a girl."

He glanced at the sun and saw that it was on its way down. A vague sadness had settled over Britton. He supposed it was because he had not seen Stella Hepburn for several days. He always felt sad and lonely when he thought of her.

"It's time we headed back to camp," he said.

He did not wait to see what the girl would do. He started the black and rode away. The girl did not follow immediately. She waited until Britton had ridden on for a short distance, then started after him. They rode like that, apart from each other, all the way back to the canyon. . . .

6

The following morning Britton rode out alone once more. He checked the canyon where the mustangs had been grazing the previous day and saw that the band was there again. Apparently, this was one of their favorite feeding grounds and so Britton laid plans accordingly.

He left the horses undisturbed and rode back out of the canyon and then began a study of the land to see how the horses could be run. Britton considered attempting to run them all the way to the canyon where they had their trap but eventually decided against it. The three of them were just not enough to handle the band on a long run like that. So Britton looked around.

He began a search of the nearby canyons and he finally came across one with a box end. If the mustangs could be driven into this one and penned, they could then be culled and the remainder driven to the camp site.

It was early afternoon by the time he reached this decision and so Britton started a check of the water holes on his way back to camp. This day he found all the barriers in place. Britton heaved a sigh of relief. He did not want trouble with Dick Rambone or anyone else. The dream was too precious to Britton. He did not like to think of its being shattered beyond repair in a fit of rage.

He had topped a rise when something prompted him to look over his shoulder and he saw the horseman below, following his tracks. A faint uneasiness chilled Britton's spine briefly as he reined in and turned the black to face the rider who was coming up the slope.

The rider was Frank Hepburn.

Hepburn was riding an orange dun with a white mane and tail and Britton found time to think that this was about the prettiest horse he had ever seen. Then he dismissed this thought and stared at Hepburn's face which was hard and stern. Somehow he gave the impression that this was the way he always looked. It was as though his face would shatter into shards if he were ever to unbend and smile.

He peered at Britton awhile. Under the gray mustache Hepburn's mouth was a thin, rigid line. The depths of his eyes looked down into a cold, unfeeling chasm. The only emotion Hepburn evinced was in the way he slapped his thighs lightly with the ends of the lines. This appeared to be done absently, however, as though the man's hands and mind were miles apart.

At last Hepburn spoke. "I see you're still in the Ladrones, Britton," he said. His voice held about as much expression as a dripping icicle.

An instant antagonism surged up in Britton. He told himself he should not let the man affect him like this, but Britton could not help himself. Nevertheless, he tried to keep his tone calm and subdued.

"I expect to be around quite a while yet," he said quietly.

"Is that right?" said Hepburn, with a touch of acid in his voice. A corner of his mouth twitched once, a revelation of the wrath he was suppressing. "I take it you're doing all right then."

"I'm not complaining."

Hepburn went on slapping his thigh, the lines making soft, fluffing sounds. His gelid eyes all the while scanned Britton from head to foot. There was arrogance in the glance, but it held something more, something like a crafty and profound speculation.

"Why did you pick this part of the Ladrones, Britton?" he asked suddenly.

The question surprised Britton and his brows went up. "This is good mustang country," he said.

"Why didn't you take the other side of the mountains?" asked Hepburn, indicating the direction with a curt nod of his head.

Britton put out an effort to keep his voice even, because wrath was beginning to run in him. "We looked it over but there are too many ranches there. The mustangs hang out here on this side."

"Aren't there any ranches here?" asked Hepburn, his voice hardening perceptibly. "Doesn't Chain Link count as a ranch?"

"We're not bothering Chain Link," said Britton, his voice taking on a growl even though he tried to keep it level.

Hepburn lifted his head a little and the sun glinted off the surfaces of his eyes. They looked very bright, like agates in a strong light. "Are you sure?" he said sharply. "Are you sure, Britton?"

This time Britton did not attempt to check the burst of anger. He went along with it, kneeing the black over a little so that it almost crowded the orange dun. Britton's face was thrust forward, the line of his jaw was stern and taut.

"Look, Hepburn," he growled, "we're only interested in unbranded mustangs. If we ever find any Chain Link horses running wild with these *mesteños*, we'll cut them out and turn them loose. Fair enough?"

Hepburn's teeth showed slightly as he allowed himself a small smile of disdain. "Will you now?" he sneered, and uttered a short, mirthless laugh.

Britton's arm was raised, the back of his hand poised to smash Hepburn across the mouth, before he became aware of it. The whole of him was atremble with wrath. He had a quick, brief vision of Stella Hepburn and it was this more than any-thing else that deterred him.

Hepburn had stiffened in surprise and anger. His eyes glittered and now his teeth bared in a definite, irate snarl. He growled something unintelligible and his right hand grabbed at the handle of the .45 at his hip.

Britton dropped his hand quickly, clutching at Hepburn's wrist as he started his draw. The barrel of the six-shooter cleared the top of the holster, but that was as far as Hepburn got it for then Britton, with a savage exertion of strength, bore down on Hepburn's wrist, shoving his arm down and to the side. At the same time Britton jabbed the black hard with a spur and the black hit the orange dun so abruptly that it shied away a little.

Britton jabbed again with the spur and the black crowded the dun and now Britton gave a hard twist to Hepburn's wrist and the man grunted with pain and the .45 dropped from his fingers. Britton gave one more vicious twist that brought Hepburn hipping around in the saddle, almost unseating him. Then Britton let go and reined the black away. He was breathing audibly, chest rising and falling almost convulsively. Sweat trickled down through the beard stubble on his cheeks. A few drops fell off his chin.

Hepburn reined the orange dun around and back so that he faced Britton. Hepburn started to speak once, lips writhing, but only choked sounds emerged from his throat. He swallowed with great effort and then he spat at the ground in front of the black. This act seemed to restore his voice.

"Get out of the Ladrones, Britton," he snarled. "Get out of them quick. If you know what's good for you, you'll get out of them tomorrow."

Hepburn glanced once at his six-shooter lying on the ground. Then with a grimace of hate and contempt he wheeled the orange dun and sent it off at a gallop. Britton watched until even the dust of Hepburn's going had vanished. Only then did he start the black for camp. . . .

The sun was westering as Britton rode into camp. He noted instantly that Lane had not come in yet. Britton realized a measure of regret as he recalled how gruff and abrupt he had been with the boy the past few days. It was none of Lane's fault.

Britton spied the three strange horses and the first fit of apprehension passed through him. His eyes narrowed as something familiar pawed at his mind for recognition. After a moment, revelation came and, with the knowledge, a sensation that was both disturbing and ominous.

He hardly glanced at the three who sat with Kyle Reeve around a blanket spread on the ground. Britton was aware that they looked at him, but he rode on to the corrals. There he unsaddled the black and rubbed it down and then gave it a feeding of grain before turning it into the enclosure.

He started back slowly and reluctantly. The old wrath had jumped back in his mind and he did not like it. It presaged too many dark and unpleasant things and heightened the realization of the futility of his dream. He regretted now that he had let the dream get such an obsessive hold on him. Life was never resolved through dreaming. Life was much too hard and brutal for such a simple and easy solution.

He went to the spring first for a drink and there he found Carmen, filling a pail with water. She threw him an apprehensive look and he saw the troubled and almost fearful glimmer in the depths of her eyes. He interpreted this as a reaction to the grim and forbidding cast of his unshaven features.

The girl filled her pail and then Britton drank from the dipper that they kept on a rock next to the spring. He had started away when something occurred to him and he went back and took the pail out of Carmen's hand. The look she laid on him was startled. Then a bit of color tinged her cheeks and he thought she was going to smile, but he turned away before finding out and carried the pail over to the fire.

Reeve and the three were still squatted around the blanket, playing poker. All four glanced up as Britton walked in, spurs mourning softly, and set down the pail. When Britton straightened, one of the four said:

"Hello, friend. Nice layout you got here."

Britton turned his glance on Mingo. The man's lean, angular face was cracked by a smile that never even came close to warming his eyes. Nothing probably ever warmed them, Britton thought.

Surratt and Gerber both nodded at Britton, but he gave no indication that he noticed this. He flicked a glance at Kyle Reeve, squatting there very quiet and withdrawn, and then returned his attention to Mingo.

"What're you doing here?" Britton asked Mingo.

The smile, which was really a grimace, left Mingo's face by degrees as though it took all the wrinkles a long time to smooth out. Mingo blinked once, then his eyes were as blank and direct as a look of the dead.

"We ran into your partner and got acquainted," said Mingo in an offhanded way. "He invited us for coffee and then we got around to a friendly game of poker to kind of pass the time. Would you care to sit in, Britton?"

"No."

The tone of it made Mingo blink again. Ben Surratt made a grunting sound as he shifted himself to a more comfortable position. Randy Gerber began to smile in a slight, taut way. Kyle Reeve just sat and watched, his face strangely empty of expression. Not even the sardonic amusement was there.

"It's just a friendly game," said Mingo. "Small stakes. Just something to while away the time."

"No."

Mingo's glassy stare shifted a moment to where the girl was poking around the fire, then it returned to Britton.

"We just mean to be sociable," Mingo said after a brief pause. "We just came to visit and talk."

"Talk about what?"

"We've already gone over it with your partner."

"Gone over what?"

Mingo lowered his stare and picked up the cards. He riffled them, his eyes averted as though he were thinking on something, and then he lifted his glance back to Britton.

"We'd like to throw in with you, Britton."

The unexpectedness of this left Britton|momentarily without words. Something pernicious began needling his mind. He remembered the dead fire of the other day and what it implied and a great uneasiness started to compete with the resentment that had risen in him.

"I wouldn't care at all for a thing like that," he said.

Gerber cleared his throat and Mingo looked at him. Gerber was still smiling in that tight way. His eyes twinkled brighter than ever. After a while, Mingo brought that dead stare back to Britton. The cards made soft, rippling sounds as Mingo went on riffling them.

"Let me explain, Britton," said Mingo. "There's a lot of mustangs here in the Ladrones. Me and my boys could set up a camp of our own, but then we'd just be competing against you. Why don't we all pitch in together? With six of us rounding up those horses, we could do a pretty thorough job. What do you say?"

"I'm not interested."

Surratt grunted again as he shifted position. The new stance permitted his holstered gun to hang free. Mingo glanced at Surratt and then at Gerber, still smiling, and then back to Britton, standing there tall and dark and grim.

Kyle Reeve sat quietly, never saying a word.

"I'm sure we'd get along pretty good, Britton," Mingo murmured.

"And I'm sure we wouldn't get along at all," said Britton, mouth tightening. "Get out!"

Mingo riffled the cards loudly. His brows went up, but that was the only expression his face registered. The glassy eyes remained blank and disinterested. "How's that?" Mingo said softly.

"You heard me. Get out, all of you!"

Mingo opened his right hand and the cards fell, scattering all over the blanket. Mingo rose slowly, his tall, lean length seeming to unfold gradually. On his feet, he came around slowly until he faced Britton squarely. Mingo's face was still expressionless.

Aping Mingo, both Surratt and Gerber rose. Surratt grunted and pressed his paunch as if settling it in place. The smile had widened on Gerber's mouth. His eyes twinkled with a burning eagerness. He moved out a little to the side until he was flanking Britton slightly. Surratt moved out in the opposite direction and Britton found himself in a whipsaw.

Reeve still sat, not moving and not saying anything, watching it all with a calm, withdrawn interest.

"You're not very sociable, are you, friend?" Mingo's voice was a shade on the hard side.

"I'm not interested in being sociable," said Britton, wrath mounting in him. "Get out of this camp and stay out!"

"What if we don't want to get out?" said Mingo.

Britton saw how it was. They had him from the front where Mingo stood and from both sides. Britton did not underestimate the menace of these men. They were hard and experienced in the ways of violence and he was quite positive that just any one of them would have been more than a match for him. The three of them together and the whipsaw besides eliminated whatever slight chance he might have had.

Nevertheless, the wrath was so great in Britton that he didn't think once of backing down. The roiling of the rage was so overwhelming that it made him heedless of consequences. His eyes glowered, the line of his jaw became stern and unbending.

"You'll get out anyway," Britton said, fury making his voice thick.

Now Mingo smiled. The stretching of his lips put a lot of wrinkles in his cheeks and revealed large, yellowed teeth. His eyes remained as dead and glassy as ever, but there was a cunning triumph in the rest of his face. He could not conceal that.

"You're calling the game, friend," said Mingo. "It's up to you to lead the first card."

Britton turned cold inside. For an instant, there was ice in his belly, then some of the chill left and he felt almost detached and observing this from the outside. His mind grasped the inevitableness of it almost impersonally and very objectively. He would die but he would take one, and possibly two, of them with him. Which one or two would they be? he asked himself.

Gerber chuckled softly and Britton felt his eyes pull toward the fellow. Gerber seemed vastly amused. He was apparently getting a big kick out of this. Someone was going to die, Gerber was obviously thinking, but it would not be him. It was then that Britton decided Gerber would be his first target. Britton drew a deep breath, tensed and prepared to go for his gun.

In this moment of prescient stillness, the sound angled in. Mingo and his partners heard it the same instant Britton did. The three froze because the noise had emanated from behind them. Britton had only to raise his glance and there he saw Lane.

The boy had come up quietly, his sorrel's hoofs making hardly a sound in the sand. Lane had gathered the implications immediately and he had taken out his six-shooter and cocked it. It was the noise of this last that had worked through the deadly silence.

"What's this?" asked Lane. His voice was stern and firm.

Mingo turned his head to look at Lane. Mingo's face had gone hard. For an instant, his eyes lost their blankness and glowed with an incandescent hate, but he masked them quickly and when he looked at the boy, Mingo's glance was bland and dead once more.

A moment Mingo studied the boy. Then Mingo's look came down and said something to each of his partners. They turned slowly until they faced Lane while Mingo diverted his complete attention to Britton.

It dawned then on Britton that this was not over yet.

Reeve still sat quietly.

Then the girl spoke up. "This has gone far enough," she said, and Britton was startled by the fury in her tone. "You're leaving here, Mingo, either under your own power or packed across your saddle. The choice is yours."

Britton saw Mingo's glance flick past him and then Mingo's face screwed up in an expression of insufferable rage. A snarling grimace wrinkled his cheeks and he uttered a small, animal sound of wrath.

Britton turned his head and saw Carmen. While

Mingo and the others had been intent on Britton, the girl had gone into the lean-to and now she stood just outside with a Winchester at her shoulder. The hammer was back and her finger was tight against the trigger; she was looking down the sights right at Mingo's heart.

Britton drew his .44. A strange excitement was running through his blood. He laid a gelid glance on Mingo. "You'd better go, Mingo," said Britton. The muzzle of his .44 pointed at Mingo's chest.

Mingo drew himself up. His breast swelled as though he were gathering breath for a torrent of words. Color darkened the wind-burned crests of his cheeks. He was a moment like that, then he expelled his breath in a lingering sigh.

"Stay out of my way, partner," said Mingo, eyes lacking any expression at all as they stared at Britton. Mingo then spun on his heel and walked over to his horse and mounted.

Surratt and Gerber did likewise. Not one of the three so much as glanced at Britton. They spurred their horses and went at a gallop down the canyon, lifting a spurning cloud of dust in their wake.

Britton watched until they passed through the entrance. Then he holstered his .44 and found that his hands were trembling. The muscles were quivering in his thighs and there was a queasy sensation in his stomach.

Lane stepped down from the sorrel. His eyes kept moving from Reeve, still sitting, to Britton and then on to the girl. "What's this all about?" asked the boy, frankly puzzled.

The girl leaned the Winchester against a rock. "Nothing, Eddie," she said, running the back of a hand over her sweating forehead.

"Nothing?" echoed the boy in astonishment. "They were all set to cut down on Steve. Do you call that nothing?"

Britton stepped to the fire and poured himself a cup of coffee. He sipped some and noted that the trembling had just about gone from his hands. Shifting his eyes, he discovered the girl staring at him in a strange, intent way. She did not avert her eyes, not even when he challenged them with a hard, direct look of his own.

"How about you, Kyle?" Lane asked suddenly. "What were you doing all the while? Why didn't you take a hand?"

The boy's words brought Britton around on his heels, spurs jingling from the abruptness of the movement. Britton's teeth were pressed tightly together, a muscle along his jaw bulged.

"Yes, Kyle," he said tautly. "What about you?"

Reeve rose with a slow deliberateness. He paused to brush some sand from the seat of his trousers and his chaps. Then he laid an innocent, inquiring glance on Britton.

"I don't follow you, Steve."

"You follow me, all right," growled Britton. "You just sat there and watched. Even after they worked me into a whipsaw, you just watched."

The corners of Reeve's mouth drew in. His eyes seemed to withdraw and he looked as though his mind had gone far away. After a while, he said:

"Listen, Steve. You've been riding roughshod over all of us of late. We've all taken it, we've taken more of it than we should have, but that don't mean you can ride roughshod over everyone." He paused while his eyes probed at Britton's face. "You were walking on pretty thin ice right there. I wasn't going to make any sudden move that would start Mingo and his boys to shooting. If it had come to a fight, I'd have backed you. You should know that, but I wasn't going to start it."

"Who's Mingo?" Britton asked abruptly. His eyes were thin and algid.

Reeve spread his hands and made a mouth. "How should I know?"

"How come he was here?"

"He just rode in and introduced himself and his pals."

"How come you're so friendly with him?"

"Friendly?" echoed Reeve, arching a brow.

"You were playing cards with him, weren't you?"

"What the hell's wrong with that?" cried Reeve. Color darkened the high points of his cheeks. "I was just passing the time. You don't gamble, Eddie don't gamble, you're both saving your money for your crazy dreams. Me, I want some fun out of life and I aim to get it while I can still enjoy it. You can live like a monk, Steve, but don't you ask that of me."

Britton's glance slitted. His heart was beating with strong, measured strokes. A fit of rage pierced his brain, but he decided to ignore it.

"You know what Mingo is, don't you?" he asked Reeve.

The nettled curving of Reeve's mouth indicated ignorance. "No, I don't," he said with a trace of ugliness. "What is he?"

"I'll give you ten to one that him and his boys are running off Chain Link cattle."

"Is that right?" said Reeve, arching his brows. He lifted a hand and tugged at his sideburns. His eyes grew very thoughtful. "Have you any proof?"

"The other day," said Britton, "I came across a fire fresh put out, a fire that looked like a branding fire. Then Mingo and his partners rode up and bummed me for some tobacco. They were the ones who'd built that fire and they were checking to see who I was. There's a lot of places in the Ladrones where cattle can be hidden. Do you get the drift now, Kyle?"

"So what?" said Reeve, carelessly. "From what I hear, Chain Link can afford to lose a few head. They got so many they won't miss them."

The muscles bulged along Britton's jaw. When he spoke his voice was hoarse with suppressed fury. "Is that what you had in mind?"

he growled. "Is that why you brought Mingo here?"

Reeve's forehead wrinkled. One eye squinted almost shut as he peered at Britton. "What the hell are you driving at?"

"You know what," said Britton, all of him tense with pent-up wrath. He had no idea how much longer he could contain, himself. "You probably figured you could get me to start rustling Chain Link cows. You figured because I'd done that down around Las Cruces that I'd do it again. Well, I'm through with that, do you hear, Kyle? I'm through with that for good."

Reeve spread his hands, face slack with bewilderment. "I had no such thing in mind. You've been pasturing on loco weed, Steve."

"I know you, Kyle," snarled Britton.

"Oh, you do, do you?" cried Reeve. Anger stiffened his lips and colored his cheeks. "Let me tell you something, Steve. I've taken about all I'm ever going to take from you. What right have you got to set yourself up like you were God Almighty and pass judgment on everyone else? You don't know a damn thing that goes on in my mind. Remember that. Remember that the next time you make a crack about me, because the next time I ain't taking it lying down. Next time you say something like that without proof to back you up we're having it out. We're having it out and, believe you me, I ain't coming out of it second best—"

7

The partners rode out the following day and went to the canyon Britton had selected for their new trap. They checked it carefully and concluded that the walls were too precipitous for the horses to climb. They then built a trap at the far end of the canyon. It was late in the day by the time they were done and they returned to camp.

They unsaddled their horses and rubbed them down and then walked back to the fire. Carmen had baked some dried-apple pie and had set the plates on a rock to cool. Reeve went over and was going to help himself, but Carmen chased him away. She laughed as she did this, but her heart did not seem to be in it. She glanced at Britton, but he had gone on to the spring to wash up. He did not once look at her.

When he came back, he noticed where the girl had strung a lariat between two trees and had hung out some clothing she had washed that day. The clothing was Britton's. He walked over there and, since the clothes were dry, took them off the line. He turned to find Carmen walking up to him.

She smiled. Her teeth looked very white against the dark color of her skin and the smile put tiny wrinkles at the corners of her eyes. "There's a button missing and a rip in the sleeve of your shirt, Steve," she said, the throatiness of her voice stirring something in him which he resented instantly. "I'll mend it for you tomorrow."

"You needn't bother," he said.

The smile died. Her face twitched as if a spasm of pain had passed through her. "It wouldn't be any bother," she said. Her eyes appeared to be pleading for something. "I'd like to do it very much."

Britton stared at her narrowly. She started to avert her eyes, then swung them back defiantly. Her lower lip thrust out a little as she caught his glance and held it.

It was Britton who lowered his eyes first. He found them passing over the smooth, bare stretch of her throat and the ripe pattern of her breasts under the blue flannel shirt and he forced his eyes on past her. Something constricted in his throat as he remembered how her hips swayed in the tight fit of the Levi's when she walked. That was all she had worn since she had come. He had no idea what she would look like in a dress.

"You needn't bother," he said again, eyes on something far away. Bitterness and loneliness made an ache in his heart. "You needn't bother washing my stuff anymore, either. I can take care of that."

"But I'd like to, Steve."

"Well, I don't want you to," he snarled, suddenly very angry, yet not knowing exactly what he was wrathful about.

His tone made her start. Fear flickered for a moment in her eyes. Then her lips paled. They looked dry. "Why do you hate me, Steve?" she whispered.

"I don't hate you."

"Yes you do. Why?"

He looked at her. Her chin was thrust up, her mouth quivered as though she were about to cry. Something uneasy stirred in Britton. It was like a portent of doom for the dream he had nurtured and cherished for so long.

"Why should I hate you?" he asked, his voice gruff.

"I don't know. That's why I'm asking you."

He could not find anything to say. He moved his eyes beyond her to where Eddie Lane sat on a rock, sipping a cup of coffee and to where Kyle Reeve was happily and noisily eating a whole plate of pie. Britton's eyes returned to the girl and still his mind found nothing to say.

"Is it because of the way I came with Kyle?" she asked. Her cheeks darkened. A trace of embarrassment tinged her tone.

Britton said nothing.

"We're married," she went on. "It's my place to be with my husband. I could have stayed in Cordova, but I love Kyle and I want to be with him and help him all I can. Is there anything wrong with that?"

The sense of loneliness deepened in Britton. The dream had never been as stark and as hopeless as it appeared right now. He was weary of doing things alone. He wanted someone to work with and work for. A tongueless cry wailed in him. Stella, it whispered mournfully, Stella. . . .

The girl's eyes were on him, grave and earnest, but he would not look at her. He did not dare look at her because she was real and he wanted some-thing like that, something that he could feel in his arms, something more tangible than the tantalizing nebulosity of a dream.

"I wish you'd tell me what it is I'm doing wrong," Carmen went on when he did not speak. "I'd like to help all I can. I'd like to be your friend. Will you let me, Steve?"

"You'd better get back to your cooking," he said gruffly. "Something's burning."

She uttered a sound of dismay and dropped back a step, searching his face for something she could not find. A moment she hesitated, scanning his features. Then she turned and was gone, running lightly.

Britton walked in slowly and carried his clothes into the lean-to. When he came out, Carmen was busy at the fire. He gave her a passing glance and moved on, troubled and restless.

He went up to the spring for a drink and when

he returned chow was ready. Carmen handed him his plate without a word or a direct look. He preferred it this way, but still it left him rather sad. He sat on a rock and ate in silence.

When he was through, he walked out to the edge of the firelight and rolled a cigarette. Then he walked out a little more. After a while, he heard footsteps behind him and when he turned his head he saw Lane coming up in the shadows.

The boy stood awhile without speaking, hands thrust into his pockets. In the darkness Britton could not read the expression on Lane's face. Nevertheless, Britton had the impression that the boy was unusually solemn and grave tonight. He was probably thinking of his Mona.

After a while, Lane said, "Why aren't you nicer to Carmen, Steve?" The words were almost blurted out.

Britton stiffened. A quick anger knifed his brain. He took a breath before speaking. "What're you talking about?"

Lane shifted uneasily on his feet. "You know what I mean. Carmen's all right. She isn't what you think she is. She's a good worker. She's— well, she's all right. Why don't you talk nice to her instead of being rough all the time?"

The tip of the cigarette glowed red as Britton drew hard on it. He blew the smoke out slowly, aware of the quick tripping of his heart. There was resentment in him and anger and a great irascibility. He tried not to heed them because he liked the boy.

"Let's not talk about it," he said quietly.

"It won't take much for you to be nice to her."

"I said let's not talk about it!"

The boy was silent awhile. His boot made a soft sound as he kicked at the ground. Then he said, "All right, Steve." His spurs sang very gently as he moved away.

Britton stood there, staring out beyond the twinkling stars. The cigarette worked down to a butt and he pinched it out and flipped it away. He turned his head for a look at the fire and he saw Reeve squatting in front of a blanket, playing solitaire. Lane had his guitar. He was sitting on a rock, strumming the instrument. Carmen came over and sat down beside the boy. He began to sing.

"As I walked out in the streets of Laredo,
As I walked out in Laredo one day . . ."

Britton shifted his attention back to the blackness beyond the stars. He tried to picture Stella Hepburn there, but her image came only with the greatest difficulty and then it wasn't too clear. Pain began in his heart when he thought that it was several days since he had seen her. She had stopped coming around. Why? Had she somehow found out about his past? Was that the reason? If that were so, then it was best that it had ended so soon. It was best that it had terminated before he had made too many plans. He should be thankful if this was how it was. Nevertheless, he found small consolation in this line of thinking.

He cocked his head to one side and tried to concentrate on the boy's singing. Carmen had joined in and they were singing together. The sad song fitted in very nicely with the way he felt, Britton thought bitterly.

" 'Get six jolly cowboys to carry my coffin,
Get six pretty girls to carry my pall;
Put bunches of roses all over my coffin,
Put roses to deaden the clods as they fall . . .' "

The wind whispered as it came down the canyon. Somewhere up there a horse trumpeted. Then the wind whispered again. Stella, Britton thought achingly. I wonder what you're doing, Stella. Stella. . . .

In the morning, the partners rode out accompanied by the girl. They checked the trap they had built the previous day and then Britton assigned positions to Reeve and Lane and the girl. After that, he entered the canyon where the mustangs fed and heaved a breath of relief when he spotted the band.

He worked his way carefully around the mustangs until he was on the other side of them. Then he charged them with the black running hard and swift. He fired his .44 and that was all the *mesteños* needed to send them into panicked flight.

Reeve and Lane and the girl picked up the band outside the canyon and steered it into the trap. A few mustangs got away, but most of the horses were penned in the box canyon. Some of the gloom lifted from Britton when he counted the horses milling there. It began to look like his dream had another chance.

They set about cutting out the culls. The girl worked along with them. Dust gathered on her face until it looked like an eerie mask with the darkness of her eyes peering out against a pale background.

By late afternoon, the last cull had been turned loose. Twenty-two horses remained. The partners selected ten of these and fitted them with clogs, which were forked sticks fixed to a front ankle with the prongs lashed together in front of the ankle. If a mustang attempted to move faster than a walk, a hind foot would interfere with the shank of the stick and trip the animal. In this fashion, they drove the ten mustangs to their camp. It was the partners' intention to return the next morning for the rest of the horses.

It was dusk when they reached their camp. After

turning the mustangs into a corral, they unsaddled their mounts and walked tiredly to the camp site. The girl washed at the spring and then she set about starting the fire. By the time she had a blaze going, Britton came up, carrying a pail of water.

"Don't fix anything fancy tonight," he told Carmen. "Stew is good enough. I'll help you with it."

She laid a long look on him, but he ignored it. He got the kettle and then began slicing potatoes into it. The girl watched him awhile, her face solemn and thoughtful. He glanced at her once and her eyes were luminous with something that put a pang in his heart and he averted his gaze angrily.

He had been too long without a woman, he told himself. This was the thing that was no good. This was the thing that made him resent Carmen. He tried not to think about it anymore, but it was too strong in him.

Something made Britton turn his head once and he caught Reeve watching him. A small, amused smile curved Reeve's mouth under the mustache. He was too far away for Britton to read the expression in his eyes, but Britton could guess it did not match the smile.

By the time the stew was cooked, night had closed in. They ate, with the wind moaning lightly down the canyon and a pair of coyotes calling to each other in the distance. They were all very tired and they turned in early.

Britton awoke before dawn and, since he was the first one up, he started the fire and put on the coffee. He was drinking some and chewing jerky when the girl came out of the lean-to, hair tousled, eyes puffy with sleep. She smiled at Britton, but he just stared at her soberly. He could hear his heart beating hard.

He told the girl he was riding out first and for Lane and Reeve to follow when they were ready. He rode out of the canyon just as dawn was breaking. In the early light the land had an eerie look and feel. Shadows lingered in the hollows and in the pockets on the sides of the Ladrones. The world lay hushed and solemn.

An uneasy prescience settled between Britton's shoulder blades and it disturbed him when he could not divine its meaning. The closer he drew to the horse trap the more pronounced this feeling became. It was not until he was ready to turn into the canyon that he noticed the barrier was open. At the same instant, three shots rang out in the canyon and then came the thunder of stampeding hoofs.

Britton tried to spur the black ahead, but he was too late. The mustangs came pouring through the opening and Britton had to jump the black out of their maddened rush to keep from being run down. A cloud of dust spumed up, for a while blocking off view of everything, and in this interval Britton drew his gun. He got the black ready and waited.

The rider was yipping shrilly as he followed in the wake of the stampeding mustangs. He did not see Britton and Britton urged the black in close. As the rider came up, Britton jumped the black ahead. The horse crashed into the rider's mount, smashing it to its knees. The rider cried out in surprise and alarm as he almost went pitching out of the saddle.

He recovered, however, and yanked his horse back up on its feet and whirled it, the gun in his hand coming up. Britton's teeth showed white in a snarling grimace. Fury writhed and spasmed in him.

"Go ahead, Rambone," he cried, his own .44 leveled at Rambone's chest. "Go on. Bring your gun up some more. Bring it up!"

Rambone froze when he saw Britton's gun and the look on Britton's face. Under the streaks of dust and sweat Rambone's features paled. His wide mouth lost its arrogance and something akin to panic glittered momentarily in his eyes. Slowly, his right hand dropped. His fingers opened and his .45 fell to the ground.

"You dirty yellow belly," snarled Britton. He sent the black ahead, crowding it against Rambone's chestnut. "You filthy, stinking coward. Get off your horse and pick up that gun."

Rambone started to back the chestnut away, but Britton kept the black moving, crowding the other horse relentlessly. Britton's face was contorted with rage. He was almost sobbing with wrath.

"Pick up that gun, I say. I've taken enough from you, Rambone. Get off your horse and pick up that gun!"

Rambone, face twitching with amazement and fear, started to wheel the chestnut and broke contact with the black. Britton swore, a sobbing sound that ripped out of his throat, and in a blaze of anger he raised his six-shooter and smashed the long barrel at Rambone's head.

Rambone saw it coming and he ducked, but not in time. The blow took him on the back of the skull and he cried out in pain. Britton chopped down again, striking Rambone on the back of the neck. The chestnut lunged violently sideways then and Rambone lost his seat. He fell, turning over in the air, and landed on his back. Rolling over, he came up on one knee and then cowered there, shielding his head with his arms.

"Pick up your gun," cried Britton, tears of wrath trickling down through the beard stubble on his cheeks. "You yellow, sneaking son of a bitch. Fill your hand!"

Rambone did not look up. He started to shake his head, still covering it with his arms.

Britton's whole body was aquiver with rage. Its insufferableness made a wadded ache in the middle of his chest. He wheeled the black and then spurred it ahead. Rambone sensed it coming and his head jerked up. When he saw how it was, Rambone's eyes widened in terror and alarm and he started to rise. The black hit Rambone with its front quarters and Rambone went sprawling, emitting a shout of fright as he did so.

He scrambled around frantically on the ground, turning as Britton whirled the black and aimed it for another rush. Rambone gained his feet this time and he tried to throw himself out of the way, but at the last instant the black clipped him again, spinning Rambone like a top before dropping him to the ground.

Britton wheeled the black once more, insensate with fury. His mind held nothing but the one raging desire to trample Rambone to death. Britton was crying audibly now. His dream had shattered again and he was crying in pain and in hate.

Rambone lunged up on his feet, face working with fear and despair. He crouched there, swaying from side to side, distended eyes full of the terrible sight of the black rushing at him. He tried to jump aside and grab at Britton's leg all at the same time, but the horse struck Rambone's shoulder and he cried out hoarsely as he went sprawling headlong in the sand.

Britton reined the black and spun it around with a savage jerk of the lines. His hate-ridden glance

141

picked up Rambone struggling to his feet. That was all Britton saw; that was all he wanted to see. He was vaguely conscious of something else, but the virulence of his rage was so immense that it permitted him no other consideration.

He spurred the black and it was then that something hit him. The black stumbled and plunged down on its front knees. The jolt was so sudden that Britton lurched forward. If he hadn't grabbed the saddle horn, he would have gone out of the kack. Cursing furiously, he pulled the black up and then wheeled it to see who had rammed him.

It was Eddie Lane.

Lane crowded his sorrel in, blocking Britton from another try at Rambone. Sobbing with wrath, Britton spun the black again and broke away this time. He aimed the black at Rambone who was racing for the shelter of some nearby trees.

"Steve!" Lane shouted. "Dammit, Steve, stop it!"

As Britton broke past, the boy threw himself out of the saddle. He caught Britton about the shoulders and his weight carried Britton out of the kack and the two of them crashed to the ground. Britton kicked and thrashed, scattering grit and dust, but the boy hung on.

"Easy, Steve," Lane was panting. "Take it easy."

With a violent wrench Britton broke loose. He

leaped to his feet, wild-eyed and raging, seeking the black. But Carmen had ridden in and caught the black's lines and as Britton started for the horse, the girl let him out of reach at a run. Britton brandished a fist at her and cursed, his whole body atremble.

Reeve sat there on his bay with his hands crossed over the horn and that amused smile on his mouth. Rambone, taut with terror, ran up to Reeve.

"Can't you do something with him?" the Chain Link foreman said, breathing in great, convulsive gasps. "Is he crazy?"

Reeve's eyes glittered and his smile widened a trifle. "You asked for it, amigo. Don't come crying to me."

"All I did was turn those mustangs loose. That's not a killing matter, is it?"

"With Steve it is." Reeve inclined forward in the saddle. "If I were you, Rambone, I'd get out of here as fast as I could."

Britton started for Rambone, but Lane placed himself in front of Britton. When Britton tried to brush past, the boy caught Britton about the waist.

"It's over, Steve," the boy panted, holding on despite Britton's furious struggles. "The horses are gone. You ain't gonna get them back by fighting with Rambone."

"I ain't fighting him," raged Britton. "I'm killing him."

"That would be fine, wouldn't it?" gasped the boy. "That sure would end everything for all of us."

Britton saw it then. The height of his wrath broke at that moment on hearing the boy's words. Britton had a vision of his dream lying in pieces, but they could be fitted together again. The dream was not irrevocably broken. If he killed Rambone as he wanted to, then the dream was gone for good. A sob racked Britton and he relaxed. On feeling this, Lane released his grip.

Rambone had caught his chestnut and mounted. He threw a taut look at Britton and then Rambone spurred his horse and went off at a rapid run.

Silence filled in. Reeve broke it when he shifted in his seat, making saddle leather squeal. Lane picked his hat up from where it had fallen and brushed the dust off before putting the Stetson on his head.

Carmen rode in now, leading Britton's black. Her eyes kept flicking at his face, then darting away. She looked pale and drawn and not a little scared.

Britton gave her a short glance and mounted. He rode off at a walk, heading back to camp, and the three watched him go. Not a word was said. . . .

8

The partners rode out to see what else they could find. They selected a section of the Ladrones they had not searched and then split up so as to cover a larger area.

On this day, Britton was riding up a long, serpentine canyon whose slanting walls were covered with copses of pine and cedar. White clouds were banking up beyond the crests of the Ladrones and the sun was very bright.

He had come across several traces of cow dung and he considered this strange for he had seen no cattle. This was quite some distance from Chain Link. Nevertheless, strays might have wandered this far for the graze was fair in the canyon. Britton gave it no more thought than that.

He had narrowed his eyes against the brightness of the day as he scanned the country for mustang signs and it was thus that he saw something winking in the sun. An intuition that he did not know he possessed prompted Britton to grab his Winchester out from the boot under his leg and then go hurtling out of the saddle. Something whined briefly and viciously just above him as he was falling and, moments later, the crack of a shot drifted down from the canyon slope.

A bullet smashed into the ground beside him as

he scrambled on hands and knees for a cluster of rocks and bushes just ahead. He heard the black snort in terror and go galloping off. Britton gained the shelter of the rocks just as a slug ricocheted off a stone with a banshee wail.

Britton lay there on his stomach, breathing fast. He could hear the hard pounding of his heart against the ground. A flurry of bullets came next, clipping twigs off the bushes and bouncing off the rocks and Britton realized there was more than one rifle up there, possibly three.

Three? Mingo, Surratt and Gerber?

Britton lay very quietly, trying to think of something. After a while, the shooting ceased. He brushed the hat from his head and rose up in a crouch. His heart was hurrying, his palms were wet where they gripped the Winchester. He levered a shell into the breech and peered through a break in the bushes.

He caught a glimpse of movement up the slope, but it was so brief that he was unable to define it. It was as if someone had just passed into a stand of cedar. Britton came up a little more and then his eyes caught that winking in the sun again and he was going down as a slug burned its way through the area just above his head.

He lay there a while as several more bullets came screeching down the slope, but this sounded like only one gun now. Then there was silence, heavy, prescient. Britton brushed sweat out of his eyes and edged along on the ground until he had changed position.

Slowly, he came up until his eyes peered above the surface of a rock. He scanned the slope above carefully and cautiously, prepared to drop at the first hint of a shot. After several moments, he saw someone break out of the cedars and run, bent over, for a group of large stones. Britton's Winchester roared, but he missed. Before he could get off another shot, a slug came shrieking down the canyon wall from another position and Britton had to go down behind his rocks.

He lay there, sweating and breathing fast and thinking. It did not take Britton long to divine what the three had in mind. He was pinned down here. He could not hope to get out. So, while one of them kept him covered, the other two were spreading out to get at him from all sides.

Britton cursed, not in despair or fear as much as from a sense of futility. He dragged himself on elbows and knees until he was in the very center of the rocks. If they wanted him, they would have to come to him. They would have a lot of cover as they worked in, but he would be waiting for them. He would get at least one of them, perhaps more. He promised himself this grimly.

Britton replaced the spent cartridges in the Winchester and then started to wait. The sun was overhead, but the bushes were high enough to cast a little shade down on him.

While he waited, his mind took up the dream again, but now it was a sad and hopeless recollection. The dream hadn't had a chance from the very moment it had been born and he should have recognized this fact. Nevertheless, the dream was still something precious and sweet. It was all that had sustained him those lonely and remorseful years in the penitentiary.

Every now and then that one gun up on the canyon wall would throw a few slugs down at Britton. He paid them no heed. He listened to their screech and whine almost absently. Then the gun would go silent. It was apparent that the purpose of these occasional bullets was to keep him pinned down.

He figured that one of the three had likely crossed the canyon to come down on him from the other side; so he edged around in his rocks and parted the bushes in front of him slightly until he could see out. For a while, he studied the other canyon wall without seeing anything. Then the flurry of movement came.

Britton raised the Winchester and aimed but held his fire. The range was too great for accuracy. When he fired, he wanted to kill. So he lowered the Winchester as the man up the slope glided behind some pines.

That gun opened up again and Britton ducked down and hugged a stone until the weapon quit. He lay there, thinking of Stella Hepburn. It was strange how the memory of her had started to fade. Not very much, perhaps, but nonetheless it was not as bright and vivid as it had once been. Still, the heartache was there. It would be there until he breathed his last.

The gun opened up once more and it was joined by another one, raking the rocks from two angles. This was the beginning of it, Britton thought. They were closing in for the kill. He gritted his teeth and waited, face gaunt and drawn. His heart tripped quickly, hurriedly, as if it realized it might soon be stilled forever.

He stirred impatiently in the narrow confines of the rocks, not daring to look while those two rifles kept bouncing slugs off the stones. Once he thought of Carmen and the way she kept stealing glances at him and he wondered that the remembrance of her should be so stark and bright.

Now a third gun joined in and Britton flinched involuntarily as he waited for the bullets to come from still another direction. Then it dawned on him that this was not so. The guns still roared, but the slugs had stopped screaming through the bushes and whining off the rocks.

Hardly daring to believe, he came up and looked and saw where that other gun was going from down the canyon. Something warned Britton and he came around quickly and saw the man on the other slope rising from behind a rock to draw a bead on him.

Britton snapped off a shot. The aim was hurried and he missed, but the slug came close enough to send the man down behind his rock. Britton threw another slug for good measure and had the satisfaction of seeing the fellow start to crawl away, heading for the pines. Britton tried two more shots that missed and then the fellow was in the trees.

Britton turned his attention to the other two guns. One of them had already quit and the third one did likewise when Britton opened up. The rifle down the canyon was still barking.

Now it stopped, also, when it became apparent that the bushwhackers were pulling out. After a while, Britton caught a glimpse of a horseman far up the canyon, riding away, and then another joined him. A little later, a third rider followed in their wake.

Britton picked up his hat and came out of the rocks. He started to look around for his black and saw where the horse had been caught by a rider coming up the canyon. The rider was Eddie Lane.

The boy's eyes were bright with anxiety. He swiftly scanned Britton from head to foot and Lane breathed an audible sigh of relief when he saw that Britton was unharmed.

Still, Lane had to be sure. "They get you anywhere, Steve?"

Britton shook his head. "Not a scratch."

Lane stared up the canyon. "How'd you get into this?"

"I was just riding along when they opened up on me."

"Were they laying for you?"

"I don't think so."

"Why'd they bushwhack you then?"

Britton paused before answering. An uneasy sensation crawled between his shoulder blades. "They tried awful hard to kill me when they found out who I was, but that wasn't the only reason they shot at me."

"What would the other reason be?"

Britton peered at Lane. "Didn't you recognize any of them?"

The boy frowned. "I didn't get too good of a look. I heard the shooting quite a way off and I rode up and when I saw your black with the empty saddle I figured it was you in the hole. So I took a hand." He stared narrowly at Britton. "Who were they, Steve?"

"I can't say for sure but I think they were Mingo and his boys."

"Mingo?" echoed Lane. He sucked in his breath softly. "Do you think this is where they're operating from? Is that why they cut down on you?"

"It could be," said Britton.

After mounting the black, he turned in the saddle and stared thoughtfully up the canyon. The uneasiness grew more pronounced in the small of his back. . . .

· · ·

Britton and Lane returned to camp together. Reeve had not yet come in. The two men cared for their horses and then walked over to the fire. Carmen had the coffee boiling.

Britton carried his cup over to a rock and sat down, cradling the cup in both hands while he stared moodily at the ground. Once he glanced up and saw the girl and Lane in earnest conversation. Carmen was staring at Britton and she averted her eyes almost guiltily when he looked at her. Lane also became aware of Britton watching and the boy broke off the talk. He took a few steps to the side and stood there, sipping his coffee slowly.

Britton emptied his cup and set it on the ground beside the rock. Carmen came over. "Would you like another cup, Steve?" Her voice sounded low and solicitous and again it stirred that something in Britton which he resented.

"Not right now," he said.

Her eyes were searching him. She bent over a little as if to see better. Tiny lines were etched around the corners of her mouth. "You all right?" she asked.

He peered narrowly up at her. "Shouldn't I be?"

She drew in her breath with a small, moaning sound. "Eddie told me about what happened. They—they meant to kill you, didn't they?"

He shrugged. "Well, they didn't."

She was about to say something but hoofbeats

sounded and Reeve came riding up. He dismounted and stretched, groaning softly. Then he said, "Take care of my horse, will you, kid? I'm bushed."

Lane threw Reeve a dark look, but the boy said nothing. He picked up the bay's lines and led the animal toward the corrals. Reeve went over and put an arm around the girl's waist and kissed her on the cheek.

He poured himself a cup of coffee and drank it. Then he walked over to Britton. Reeve took out the makin's and rolled a cigarette, his face expressionless. He licked the paper, smoothed the cylinder and placed it in his mouth.

"Find anything, Steve?"

"Not a sign. What about you?"

"I spotted a couple of *manadas* south of where you were looking. There are some middling broncs in them."

Britton was staring steadily at Reeve. "Mingo and his boys bushwhacked me today, Kyle," Britton said quietly. "If Eddie hadn't come up, I wouldn't be here now."

Reeve struck a match and lighted his cigarette. He exhaled a cloud of smoke that drifted up in front of his eyes. "Mingo's a bad customer, Steve," said Reeve. "You shouldn't have riled him the other day."

Britton's glance had not left Reeve's face. "Didn't you hear any shooting?"

"You know I was too far away for that."

"Were you?"

The focus of Reeve's eyes sharpened as they stared down at Britton. Something wicked glinted momentarily in Reeve's glance, then was gone. One end of the tawny mustache lifted in a tic as a corner of his mouth twitched.

"What're you trying to bring up now?" he asked. His tone was heavy and sullen.

"I'm not bringing up anything," Britton said evenly. "I'm only saying what happened—and what didn't."

Reeve took a deep drag and blew out a billowing cloud of smoke. Defiance lay in the taut lines of his face. "I haven't seen Mingo since the day he was here. If you claim I have, then you're a liar!"

Britton's glance still had not wandered from Reeve's features. "I'm not calling you anything," said Britton, "right now. I just thought I'd let you know."

Reeve made an angry gesture and turned sideways. The look he threw out of the corner of his eyes at Britton was nettled and irate. Reeve appeared about to say something, but Carmen called out that chow was ready. Reeve spun on his heel and went over to the fire where he helped himself first. The girl filled a plate and held it up to Britton as he walked in.

Reeve snarled, "Why didn't you carry it over to him? You always do."

Britton threw a sharp look at Reeve but said nothing. When Britton glanced at the girl, she flushed. Then she started filling Lane's plate. Britton returned to the rock and began to eat.

When they were through, Lane helped the girl carry the plates and utensils to the spring and helped her wash them. They came back chattering like two excited, happy children.

They seated themselves beside the fire and Lane began telling Carmen about his Mona. The girl listened with her knees drawn up and her arms clasped around her legs and her head cocked to one side. Now and then she would nod approvingly and there was a small, wan smile on her mouth which suggested that she might relish a dream like that for herself.

Reeve sat in front of the lean-to, smoking one cigarette after another, that half smile curving his mustache. Now and then he would glance at Britton, then at Lane and the girl, then out into the night at something secret that only he could see.

Britton sat morosely on his rock. Tonight, somehow, he felt sadder and lonelier than ever before, even more forsaken than those grim nights in the penitentiary. His eyes kept pulling back to the girl and he did not want them to. Every time he looked at her a sense of hunger rose in him and it was no good.

He tried to think, desperately, of Stella Hepburn and the dream. Visions of both came, but he found no pleasure in them, probably because after all they were only phantasmal things. He was growing impatient. He wanted something real, something more tangible than the nebulousness of a dream.

He wanted a home and a good woman. He, an ex-convict, wanted a good girl like Stella. Stella. . . .

9

Britton emerged from the pines and there ahead he saw the black stallion which young Hepburn called Midnight. Britton reined in and watched narrowly. The wind was in his face, carrying his scent away from the stallion, which was sniffing at the barrier around the water hole.

Britton edged the black back into the pines and went on watching from there. He scanned the surrounding country and after a while he spied young Hepburn come over a rise in the distance. However, the boy was approaching from the wrong direction with the wind at his back bearing his scent on ahead to the stallion.

Britton wanted to cry out, but that would have warned the stallion and then Britton's voice would not have carried as far as the boy. The stallion's neck arched, his ears pricked up. Then he trumpeted a cry of fright and alarm. He wheeled and thundered away, hoofs raising a clatter like a rolling drum.

Britton watched young Hepburn ride disconsolately up to the water hole. There was dejection in the shape of the boy's shoulders. They squared, however, when Britton came riding up. A smile crossed the boy's tired face.

After exchanging greetings, Britton said, "We'll

open up this hole, Bob, because he looks thirsty. We've got a trap in a canyon over that rise and if you can run him in there you'll have him. How does that sound?"

The boy's face lit up. "Aren't you using the trap?"

"Not right now."

"Do you think Midnight will come back here?"

"Let's get the fence down and then wait. That's the only way to find out."

Hepburn was nervous with excitement as they worked. A feeling of pity passed through Britton and somehow he wasn't so lonely anymore. He had been too wrapped up in himself. He wasn't the only one in the world with troubles and disappointments. A man seldom ever got everything he yearned for, Britton told himself. Life just wasn't that kind.

When they had the barrier out of the way, they rode over to the height of the rise and Britton pointed out the mouth of the canyon. Sight of it put a bit of rancor in Britton's heart for it made him recollect his run-in with Dick Rambone. Britton suppressed the remembrance, however, and concentrated on his explanations to the avidly listening boy.

"You wait in the pines," he told young Hepburn, "and I'll wait over there among those boulders. The wind will be in your favor if Midnight comes. Let him get his fill of water and then start him running and when he comes over the rise I'll pick him up and aim him for the canyon. If we can keep him between us, we should be able to steer him in there." He peered thoughtfully at the boy. "That is, if you don't mind me helping you?"

Hepburn's eyes were bright. There was a trace of awe and even worship in them, which filled Britton with a slight embarrassment. "There's no one I'd rather have helping me, Steve."

Britton watched until Hepburn disappeared into the pines. Then Britton rode over to the group of boulders which reared in irregular patterns covered with scrub growth. He rolled a cigarette and started to wait.

He told himself once that this was silly, that he should be going about his own work. Then he got to thinking that a day did not make much difference in the final attainment of his dream. If he ever achieved it, one day more or less would in no measure lessen the enjoyment of it.

The sun passed the meridian and Britton stirred restlessly in the saddle. However, he had learned patience a long time ago and he went on waiting. He wondered several times how young Hepburn was taking it. The boy, too, had learned patience or he would not have stayed after Midnight all this time.

Finally, Britton heard the shot. He came up alert in the saddle, heart quickening. A little later he heard the sound of running hoofs and then the stallion burst over the rise and hard on the horse's heels raced the boy on his roan.

The stallion started to veer away, but Britton spurred the black. When the stallion saw this he turned in the other direction but Hepburn had sent the roan ahead with a burst of speed and the stallion had no choice but to straighten out.

They thundered across the flat with young Hepburn yipping shrilly in excitement and exultation. Britton had to grin at the sound. The stallion ran hard, legs working like pistons, tail straight out and mane flying. The black on one side and the roan on the other kept the stallion pointed and he raced into the canyon.

When the stallion was penned and Britton had closed the gate, young Hepburn tossed his hat in the air and laughed with glee. He was so excited that it was a while before he could talk.

A warm glow filled Britton's heart as he watched Hepburn. When the boy could speak, he said, "I'll move my camp here. There's enough graze for Midnight and I can haul water for him from the spring. I'll start right in breaking him. What do you think, Steve?"

Britton nodded. "That sounds just fine."

Worry entered the boy's eyes. "You think Midnight can be broken?"

"I don't see why not," said Britton. "You've got lots of time so use it. You can break a horse with force or you can gentle him. It all depends on what you want with Midnight. If you want him for your own and you want him to respect and like you, you've got to be patient with him. Take your time. You can do it."

The boy started to say something but his eyes went beyond Britton and Hepburn broke off abruptly. Britton turned and what he saw stilled his heart for a moment. The rider coming into the canyon was Stella Hepburn.

"Stella, Stella," Hepburn cried as the girl rode up, "I've got Midnight. I've got him here in the trap and he can't get out. I finally got Midnight, Stella!"

The girl dismounted. Color was very bright in her cheeks and her eyes danced.

"Steve helped me," the boy said proudly. "If it wasn't for him, I never would've got Midnight."

"Oh, Steve," the girl cried with a burst of exuberance, "I knew you'd help him."

It came so suddenly that at first Britton was startled. She turned toward him impulsively and all at once her arms were around him and then her lips were brushing his lightly. Then he felt her go rigid as though she had only too late realized what she had done. Her face drew back a little and all the excitement drained out of it and it became very grave.

Britton felt his throat fill. Yearning was a knife-edged ache in his heart. Her arms started to drop away from around him and sadness and the old sense of futility possessed Britton. She was not for him, something cruel and mocking told him, she would never be for him.

A moment she seemed to hesitate, eyes wide and solemn as they searched his face. Then Britton felt her arms tighten about him, fiercely this time, and his head came down and his mouth found hers, and now everything else went passing heedlessly by.

When he lifted his head, she still held him close. Both of them had forgotten young Hepburn who stood by in embarrassed silence.

"Stella," Britton said huskily, keenly aware of the racing of his heart. "It was so long since I'd seen you. I didn't think you'd ever come anymore."

"I wanted to," she whispered. "You don't know how much I wanted to."

"Why didn't you then?"

"They wouldn't let me."

"Who wouldn't let you?" A deep and dark resentment roiled in him.

She averted her eyes and looked down. "Father said you were no good for me. When I told him I would keep on seeing you anyway, he wouldn't let me leave Chain Link anymore." Her glance rose and defiance glittered in it. "But today I rode away without telling him. I was coming to see you, Steve. Don't you believe me?"

His throat was too full for him to speak at that instant. He could only stare at her while his heart raced on, prodded by a mixture of unbelief and happiness. Now was the time to tell her, a voice insisted in him. Now was the time to lay his dream in front of her. If she cared anything at all about him, his past should not matter, and if it did, then that would be the end of it and he could stop tormenting himself with doubts and uncertainties.

"Stella," he said, and then reluctance gripped him and he could not go on.

"Yes?" she said, eyes searching his face. She could tell that something was troubling him and this brought out a small frown.

His tongue seemed thick and awkward in his mouth. It was as though he had never used it before this moment. Suddenly he was afraid to go on for what might lie ahead. If revelation of his past should turn her from him—

He closed his mind to this possibility and plunged on. "There's something I want to tell you, Stella."

"Yes, Steve?"

"It's about me."

She said nothing, but in her eyes he read tenderness and encouragement. He swallowed and was about to proceed when young Hepburn said sharply, "Stella!"

The tone of it snapped both the girl's and Britton's heads up. She tensed and sucked in her breath and then, hastily, she took her arms from around Britton and stepped away from him. She stood there, face shocked and paling, watching the horseman riding into the canyon.

Young Hepburn's features were drawn and grim. He mounted his roan and rode away before the other came up and, somehow, Britton did not like to see this although he could not blame the boy.

Frank Hepburn reined in his orange dun and for a while his hard gaze watched his son riding away. Not a flicker of emotion, however, crossed the Chain Link owner's face. It was like a mask carved out of stone for all the warmth it held, even when he shifted his eyes and glanced down at his daughter.

"Apparently I didn't make myself clear to you, Stella," he said in a chill tone. "Get on your horse. We're going back to Chain Link."

Without hesitation, the girl started to obey. Wrath and resentment were growing in Britton. "You don't have to go, Stella, if you don't want to," he said sharply.

A sudden diffusion of rage darkened Hepburn's features. He jumped the orange dun ahead, crowding the horse up against Britton so that for an instant Britton teetered off balance.

"Will you stop interfering with my family?" shouted Hepburn.

Fury clawed at the fringes of Britton's brain. He took a step back to regain his balance and as Hepburn crowded the dun some more, Britton reached up and grabbed the bridle. With a savage jerk, he swung the dun half around. Britton's eyes burned.

"Listen, Hepburn, you're not pushing me around like you do your son and daughter," he growled.

"Why, you filthy saddle tramp," snarled Hepburn. "I'll teach you to mind your tongue!"

He started to urge the dun ahead. Britton dropped his hand to his gun and his eyes speared Hepburn's wrathful countenance. Britton's teeth bared. He was remembering the other times he had met this arrogant, overbearing man and how each encounter had inspired in him a resentment that was ugly and hateful. He and Hepburn would have it out someday, that fact seemed inevitable, so they might as well have it out right now.

Just then the girl ran up. She caught Britton's arms. "Steve," she cried. "Please, Steve."

The anger started to ebb in Britton then. A sudden realization struck him that this was all wrong. He would get nowhere by fighting Hepburn. He was the father of the girl Britton loved. As much as Britton loathed the man, this was a fact he could not deny or overlook. So Britton swallowed his wrath and resentment and released his hold on the bridle.

For an instant, it appeared as though Hepburn would spur the dun to run Britton down. Rage burned with incandescent brightness in Hepburn's eyes. The muscles twitched at the corners of his mouth. Then, with a visible struggle, he got himself in hand. The stony arrogance returned to his face.

"Will you get on your horse and leave, Stella?" said Hepburn. His glance never left Britton.

The girl threw Britton a pleading look which he hardly noticed for he kept watching Hepburn. She went over to her palomino and mounted. She laid another look on Britton and then, white-faced, rode down the canyon.

Britton stood there, listening to the strong pounding of his heart. His hand still gripped the handle of his .44. He was asking himself, when would the constant thwarting of all his plans end?

Hepburn lifted the lines in his left hand and turned the orange dun until it stood sideways to Britton. The look Hepburn sent down was long and insolent.

"I want to tell you just this one thing, Britton," he said coldly. "Forget my daughter. She is already spoken for. In one month she is going to be married to Dick Rambone. . . ."

10

In the days that followed, Britton grew even more bitter and morose. He drove himself mercilessly. Only in work could he find some measure of relief from the tormenting remembrances, but even this was not enough. Somehow, memory of the disillusionment and hurt angled in to him no matter how hard he tried to lose himself in what he was doing.

The black beard stubble lengthened on his face, but the added growth could not conceal the growing gauntness of his cheeks. His eyes took on a chill, withdrawn look. He never smiled and he spoke seldom.

The partners had run two more bands into the canyon. After cutting out the culls, they set about breaking the rest. Britton was always the first one up, rising invariably before dawn, and he stayed at the corrals until darkness made further work impossible. Lane remonstrated with Britton several times, but Britton ignored the boy. Reeve, recognizing Britton's truculent temperament, prudently made no effort to interfere.

On this day, the dun threw Britton for the second time and he landed badly. When he started to rise, his knee buckled and he went sprawling, grimacing with hurt. Lane came running up while Reeve went and roped the dun.

Britton sat up and drew up his leg and began feeling his knee. The boy bent over him, face anxious. "What's wrong, Steve?"

"Just a bump on the knee," said Britton. He glanced to where Reeve had roped the dun. "I'll top him this time."

Favoring the leg, he rose to his feet. Lane reached out a hand to steady him, but Britton brushed it away. He took a step and winced with pain when his weight came down on his left leg.

"You better knock off," said Lane. "Me and Kyle will handle it the rest of the day."

Britton took another step. He clenched his teeth to keep the flash of hurt from showing on his features. Even so, he had to stop and suck in a breath before speaking.

"I can still ride."

"That's not the point." Lane's voice had turned hard. "You go rest that knee."

Britton started hobbling toward the dun. "I said I can still ride."

The boy reached out and grabbed Britton's shoulder, halting him. Britton tried to brush the hand away, but Lane just dug his fingers in deeper. They were like steel now.

"Dammit, Steve," the boy cried, "you get thrown again the shape you're in and chances are you'll bust something and be laid up for good. Where will we be then? We'll never get through with this damn job if that happens. Why don't you look at it that way?"

The pain was a throbbing ache that reached up to Britton's brain. Even his stubborn insistence could no longer deny it. Weariness numbed every nerve in his body. He was beginning to feel that if he were to drop down on the hard floor of the corral, he could fall right off and sleep.

He glanced truculently at Reeve, but he was staring at something across the canyon, face empty of expression. When Lane saw Britton hesitating, the boy went on:

"All you need is a little rest, Steve. Tomorrow you'll be as good as new. You bump that knee again today and you can't tell how long it will take you to get over it. How about it?"

Britton looked at Lane. The boy's face was taut with solicitude. His eyes were troubled and anxious. It was plain that he could not understand what had come over Britton of late and this inability to comprehend was hurting the boy.

For the first time in several days Britton smiled. It was just a small parting of the lips, but still it was a smile. "All right, Eddie."

"Good," exclaimed Lane.

He held Britton's left arm as he limped across the corral and while Britton did not need this aid he made no move to take Lane's hand away. Britton stepped through the corral gate and

Carmen was there. She had been watching the partners work.

There was concern in her glance as she looked at Britton and all this did was stir up the old resentment in him. He averted his eyes and started down the canyon, aware that Carmen was following.

Once he stumbled and almost went down. The girl came up quickly and caught him under the armpit and for a brief moment all his weight rested on her. He was instantly aware of the warm firmness of her body and a sharp ache lined the walls of his throat. Then he got his good leg under him and he straightened, but she still held on to his arm.

They went the rest of the way like that. Britton started once to disengage her grasp from his arm, but when he touched the cool fingers of her hand something deterred him. After a moment, he took his hand away.

She didn't let go until they reached the lean-to. She ducked inside and came out with Britton's blankets and unrolled them.

"You lie down," she told him, voice low and husky.

Britton eased himself down on the blankets, wincing, but after he straightened out his leg the pain eased up. Carmen was starting the fire. When the blaze was going, she put on the coffee and then came over to Britton, who was trying to take off his boots. He had managed the right one, but the left was giving him trouble.

"Here, I'll help you," said the girl.

Placing her back to him, she took his boot between her knees, but it would not come off. Britton, without thinking, set his right foot against her rump and pushed. He pushed harder than he had intended. The boot came off abruptly and the girl catapulted ahead and went sprawling. She rolled over and bounced to her feet like a rubber ball, holding the boot in both hands and laughing merrily.

Seeing her like this, all aglow with laughter, did something to Britton. The gloom lifted suddenly from him and he laughed too. Her face was flushed. The dark, short-cropped hair was all tousled up and her teeth flashed very white.

Something stirred in Britton. Its insistence sobered him and the old ache returned to his heart. His eyes looked away to the far distances. The girl saw this and she became grave too.

She walked up and dropped down on her knees beside him. "What is it, Steve?" Her voice was low and gentle.

He brought his eyes back and stared at her. Now that she was close, he could see the sharp indentation the scar made in the skin and flesh of her cheek. Sight of this arrested him for an instant. He did not speak.

"What's wrong, Steve?"

171

"Nothing's wrong," he growled, almost overwhelmed by a sudden irritableness.

"What's on your mind?"

His jaw bulged as he struggled to suppress his resentment. He lapsed into sullen silence, hoping that she would go away.

The girl shook her head sadly. "It's no good, Steve. It's no good at all."

Mingled with the anger and miserableness in Britton was the swift running of futility and despair. He tried not to heed them, but there was something ruthless and cruel in the way they persisted. He could not shake the conviction that he had been licked right from the start. He should have known better than to pin his hopes on the evanescent quality of a dream.

"What's no good?" he growled at her.

"Eating your heart out like this."

"Where did you get a crazy idea like that?"

Her eyes misted over. "You can tell me, Steve. Get it off your chest. You'll feel better if you do."

He started looking down the canyon. Bleakness lay in the wrinkles at the corners of his eyes. The black beard stubble accentuated the hard, bitter cast of his mouth.

"Is it your prison record?" she asked.

He looked at her sharply, viciously. She evinced a small start, but this did not deter her.

"It's nothing to be ashamed about," she went on, lips a trifle pale. "You made a mistake and you paid for it, but now you've changed." She reached out a hand and laid it on his arm. He glanced down and somehow his eyes were held there by the long, slim look of her fingers. "You're one of the finest, straightest men I've ever known."

She paused as if waiting for him to say something and when he remained silent, she went on, "I know what you want, Steve. Eddie told me how much you want a ranch of your own. He also told me about—about Stella Hepburn."

Britton gave a start and she noticed it. "I know you never talk about her, but Eddie knows how it is and so do I and I suppose so does Kyle. That's what you've got on your mind, isn't it?"

Britton's eyes narrowed. Wrath was building up in his chest again. "Leave her out of it."

"Eddie says she's a fine girl," Carmen continued, "and I believe Eddie. But she's not your kind, Steve. Don't you see? Not because of your record, but because of other things. If she cared anything about you, your past wouldn't mean a thing to her, but that isn't all. She's a different kind altogether from you. She's led a different life. She's used to things you could never give her. You need someone more like yourself."

"Someone like you?" he said with faint derision.

Her eyes grew wet. "Would someone like me be so terribly bad for you?" she said, voice barely above a whisper. "Would that be such a bad thing for you?"

The cruel amusement died in him. In its place had come something which he could not openly define. It was something troubling and confusing and exasperating. It left him feeling strangely wrought up inside.

In her earnestness she had bent toward him. She was so close he could smell the strong scent of wood smoke in her hair and the odor of horse sweat in her clothes. He looked down and noticed where there was a burn on the back of her left hand. That strange something, verging now on eagerness, kept mounting in him.

He thought of it as a purely animal sensation. It could be nothing else because she was not something that he regarded as sweet and fine. It had never entered his mind to consider her as a part of the dream. But he had been thinking about her, thinking in a sordidly hungry way, all these lonely days and nights. Up to now he had been able to dismiss the desire because the dream had been foremost in his yearning. Now the dream was a vague, uncertain thing; but she was real.

He grabbed her suddenly. He felt her go rigid with surprise. Her eyes widened and her head dropped back, lips parted in wordless alarm. Then he had pulled her against him and, because he hated her as much as he wanted her, he felt no need to be gentle.

He bruised his lips down on hers and on the instant they were cold and stiff, and then he felt her surge up against him and her arms embrace him fiercely and through the heedless heat of the moment he had time to realize that this was not exactly as he had wanted it. He had wanted her to struggle against it, but she was going along and this became a bittersweet thing for him.

After a moment, however, he felt the change in her. She got her hands between herself and him and through sheer force she pushed herself a little away and as their mouths parted she was breathing hard.

"No, Steve, no," she moaned.

He still clung to her. He tried to reach her mouth again, but she averted her face.

"No, Steve. Kyle. Please, Steve. Kyle can see us."

That broke the spell for Britton. As strong as the desire was, this was something that surmounted it. The rush was abruptly gone from his blood and distaste began in him. She gave another small push that broke her free of his grip and then she rose to her feet and stumbled over to the fire where she got down on her haunches with her back to him.

Britton sat there, listening to the audible sound of his breathing, his eyes fixed on her. Though he watched her a long time, she never turned once to face him. . . .

After a while, Britton started flexing his knee. It did not pain so much anymore. So he rose to his feet and tested it and found it supported his weight quite well. After several steps, he sat down and drew on his boots. Then he walked over to the spring and sat down on the rock and smoked and thought.

A little before sundown, Reeve and Lane walked in from the corrals. Lane went directly to the spring to wash up.

"How's the knee, Steve?" asked the boy.

"All right."

They returned to the fire together. Reeve finished a cup of coffee. His face looked rather strained with the lips thinner than usual and a bright glitter in his yellow eyes. He caught Carmen as she passed by and pulled her toward him. When she demurred, Reeve swore savagely.

His lips parted in a ferine snarl and he brought the back of his hand across the girl's face. The sound of it was as sharp as a gunshot. The girl cried out and stumbled away, covering her face with her arms as Reeve advanced on her, hand poised for another blow.

"I'll learn you," snarled Reeve, and clouted her alongside the head. The blow tore a cry out of the girl and sent her reeling.

Britton's fists balled. He experienced a sweep of rage which he could not ignore. As Reeve raised his arm to strike the girl again, Britton said:

"Leave her be, Kyle!"

"Oh?" cried Reeve. He came around with his

arm still held high, face contorted in an exaggerated grimace of surprise. "Did you say something, Steve?"

"I said leave her alone."

Reeve's arm came down. With both hands, he hitched up his flaring chaps. The sneer on his mouth was deliberate and ugly. "You sure are a great one for telling other people how to behave, aren't you? Everything everyone else does is wrong. Everything you do is right. Well, that don't hold with me." He spat insolently in front of Britton's boots.

"You're a great one for talking about right and proper when it concerns other people," Reeve went on, the words running in a strong, truculent current. "What do you call it when it concerns you? I saw everything from the corral. What did you call that, Steve? You did everything but straddle Carmen and if you'd done that it wouldn't have surprised me a bit. Was all that right and proper? Was all that right and proper because *you* were doing it?"

"Kyle," said Britton, taking a step ahead, face glowering, "shut up or this is the end of it. Mind me, Kyle."

Reeve made an obscene observation to this. Wrath broke shrieking and overwhelming in Britton's brain. He bore down on Reeve with a rush, but Reeve had been expecting it and Britton's knee was still a little stiff. Reeve stepped to the side as Britton swung and then Reeve lashed out himself, catching Britton alongside the head and Britton went sprawling.

He heard Carmen cry out as he fell and then he went down among some kettles and pans with a clatter. Reeve came rushing in with boots and spurs aimed and Britton rolled violently to get out of the way. That was how Reeve fought, Britton thought. Get a man down and then slash him with those sharp spurs and stomp him with the boots. So Britton rolled as fast as he could, but Reeve came right along with him.

Britton slammed into a rock which stopped and briefly stunned him. Reeve cried out in triumph and lunged in, boots high. With a frantic twist, Britton averted his head. He heard the solid thud as Reeve's boots hit the ground. Then Britton was reaching out. Reeve started to jump back, but he was not quick enough.

Britton's arms closed about Reeve's legs. Breath panting in his throat, Britton gave a jerk that ripped a cry of alarm out of Reeve as his balance began to teeter. Britton jerked again and Reeve fell.

He started to roll as soon as he hit the ground. Britton made a dive for Reeve but missed. Then Reeve was rising to his feet and coming around in a crouch, all in one swift, continuous flow of motion. Britton came up too. His knee twinged once, but he paid it no heed.

Britton started a roundhouse swing which Reeve blocked, but Britton bore right on in and drove his left fist into Reeve's middle. Reeve grunted with pain, face grimacing, and fell back a step. Britton smashed him in the middle again and when Reeve's arms fell, Britton straightened quickly and hit Reeve on the jaw.

Reeve emitted a hurt sound and fell back another step. His fancy spurs tangled with the ground and he tripped and went sprawling. The fire was behind him and he came down on the edge of the blaze. A shower of sparks flew up, but Reeve rolled away before the fire hurt him. One hand reached out and grabbed a stick and when Reeve came up on his feet he was brandishing the piece of wood.

Reeve stood his ground a moment, then began advancing on Britton. Britton fell back, eyes on that club moving in menacing circles in front of Reeve. The breath was fast and hard in Britton's throat. Rage stormed in him. All he could see was the final, irreparable dissolution of all his dream and he could have wept with fury and frustration.

Abruptly, Reeve lunged, club held high. Reeve's eyes distended with a sudden sense of brutal triumph and he shouted with wrath and bestial glee as he started to come down with the club. Britton threw himself headlong, aiming for Reeve's middle. A flash of pain shrieked through Britton's brain as the club hit him high on the shoulder. Then he was slamming into Reeve.

Reeve gasped retchingly and the club flew from his grip. He caught Britton about the neck as he fell and carried Britton to the ground with him. Reeve started to tighten his hold, but with a violent wrench Britton twisted his head free. His ears were stinging, breathing was a torment.

Reeve brought a knee up, grinding it into the flesh of Britton's belly. Pain choked Britton for a moment. He experienced a sensation of falling to great depths and then his brain cleared and he found Reeve on him, both hands about his neck, thumbs digging in cruelly.

He had a good look at Reeve's face now, only inches above his. Reeve's teeth were bared. His eyes glowed with a malevolent hate. Drops of spittle kept falling out of his mouth.

Breath would no longer pass through Britton's throat. A great ball of pain was forming in his chest. He kept clawing at Reeve's wrists, but he lacked the strength to break Reeve's grip. The world began to blacken and reel in Britton's eyes.

Desperately, he reached up and grabbed Reeve's hair with both fists and yanked hard. Reeve howled, but his strangling hold would not yield. Britton yanked again with all the strength he had left. Reeve's agony was a blast that stunned Britton's eardrums and the constricting hold was gone from around his throat.

Britton pulled once more and dragged Reeve,

screaming, to the ground. Here, however, Reeve rammed an elbow into Britton's stomach that left him gasping and caused him to let go of Reeve's hair. Reeve spun himself on his rump, legs held high, and when they were over Britton's face, Reeve lashed down with the sharp rowels of his spurs.

With a sense of panic, Britton watched the spurs. He flung up his arms and managed to get them on the other side of Reeve's boots and pushed enough to divert them a little. Britton gave a violent twist that carried his face out of the way, but still the spurs slashed down on his shoulder.

The pain of it was a stinging sensation at first. Britton came up on his feet, raging. Reeve was bending over to pick up the club again. Britton rushed as Reeve straightened and smashed both fists into Reeve's face. Reeve moaned with pain and fell back. He started to bring up the club.

Britton drove in. He slammed a fist into Reeve's midsection that doubled the man over and when Reeve was like that, Britton brought up a knee and smashed it against Reeve's jaw. Reeve groaned sickeningly and stumbled to the side, still bent over, hands clutching his stomach. Britton clasped both fists together and brought them down with all his remaining strength on the back of Reeve's neck.

Reeve fell, sprawling headlong. He got his elbows under him and started to push himself up, but when he was about a foot above the ground his strength deserted him and he fell, face grubbing the earth. He lay there very still.

Britton stumbled over to the spring. The water revived him and after a while his breathing started to come easier. Now he began to feel stiff and sore all over. He had hurt his knee again, although in the fury of the battle he had not been aware of it, and he limped as he returned to the fire and went over to a rock and sat down.

Reeve was sitting up, shaking his head as though to clear it. After a while, he rose to his feet and started for the spring. He walked bent over slightly as though something pained him greatly inside. He walked in the same fashion when he returned.

He got his bedroll and lay down on it in front of the lean-to. He did not eat supper. He just lay on his stomach with his chin propped on one hand. For a long time he watched Britton. The hate in Reeve's eyes was naked and unrelenting.

In the morning, Reeve and Carmen were gone. . . .

11

All that morning Britton had been feeling rather uncomfortable. It was nothing, however, that he could put his finger on. It was more of an intuition than anything else and he tried to shrug it from him, but it would not go.

He and Lane had broken all the mustangs in the days that Reeve had been gone and now they were riding out to find some more. Now and then Britton thought of Reeve and how the man had left in the middle of the night without a word of farewell, and Britton knew a bit of sadness and regret. However, it was best this way. He and Reeve could no longer get along together. It was best for both that they had parted, even though Britton needed another man. He'd make out, however, Britton told himself.

He reined in the black and gazed at the mouth of the canyon ahead. Apprehension fluttered in the small of his back and he cursed softly, both in irritability and consternation.

He fashioned a cigarette and smoked it, all the while studying the canyon, troubled by that something whose vague insistence filled him with a faint misgiving. The land looked peaceful and serene. The sunlight was very clear and beyond the mountain peaks the clouds were piled up in white tiers.

When he was done with the cigarette, Britton pinched out the butt and flipped it away. He rode into the canyon, wondering again that he should feel so uneasy. A gust of wind came mourning down the canyon and flung several particles of grit into his face.

The apprehension deepened when he came to young Hepburn's camp. The ashes of the fire were long dead. The crude corral the boy had erected was empty. Both his roan and the stallion he called Midnight were gone.

Another gust of wind created small dust devils as it swept the canyon floor. A feeling of dread crawled among Britton's entrails. He could not understand why he should experience this and the sensation made him angry.

He told himself he was like a panicky old woman, reading dire omens in perfectly natural things. There was an explanation behind all this. Young Hepburn had likely broken Midnight and had finally returned to Chain Link. But why had the boy not visited Britton first?

Britton cursed vexedly and rode the black out of the canyon. He had enough to think about his own future without concerning himself with the troubles and foibles of others. So he put his mind back on the dream to see if that would help lessen the gloom.

The dream was not very good anymore. He had had to rebuild it. He had had to discard certain parts of it and the elimination of these had left a sour, vapid taste to the dream. The woman was gone from it. The ranch was still there, but not the woman. Loneliness had taken her place.

He passed deep into the Ladrones and here he found mustang sign again. These horses, however, were too far from their camp. They would have to shift their base here if they were to go after these. So Britton started looking around for a likely spot.

He found a canyon with a narrow entrance which could easily be closed off. Riding up the canyon, he found water and graze, but the canyon was open at both ends. It narrowed considerably at one place, however, and it could be sealed off there and a trap built against the precipitous walls. With that in mind, Britton rode back.

He was just emerging from the canyon when he spotted the horseman coming hell-for-leather toward him. Britton reined in sharply, heart quickening. The rider came on with heedless haste, leaving a great cloud of dust in his wake.

The rider was Eddie Lane.

Lane pulled his sorrel to a sliding halt. The horse was blowing, lather flecked its heaving flanks. It stood there on spraddled, trembling legs while the boy wiped sweat off his face with a sleeve of his shirt.

"Thank God I found you, Steve," said Lane, his voice hoarse.

Britton's heart was hammering in uneasy speculation. "What is it, Eddie?"

"All hell's broke loose, Steve. You've got to get out of the Ladrones. You've got to get as far away from here as you can!"

Something died in Britton. He did not know what it was. He knew only that something was gone irrevocably, leaving behind it only sadness and pain.

"What're you talking about, Eddie?"

The boy was half sobbing. "That goddam Kyle. The no-good, rotten son of a bitch. You should've killed him, Steve. I should've helped you kill him."

Dread lay in the chill, constricting walls of Britton's throat. Dread lay in the ice in his belly and in the spasmodic fluttering of the muscles in his thighs.

"What's Kyle done now?" asked Britton, thinking instantly of Mingo and Surratt and Gerber.

"It was Stella who told me," said Lane, and Britton felt his heart go cold at the sound of her name. "She's riding the Ladrones to warn you too. We split up because we felt we had a better chance of finding you then. It's a good thing I picked up your tracks before Chain Link did."

That shroud of ice would not leave Britton. His lips were stiff and dry. When he swallowed, his throat ached. "What's Chain Link got to do with this?"

"Everything," cried Lane. "Chain Link's on the warpath. Bob Hepburn is dead!"

It was like a mountain had shattered over Britton and each and every ponderous fragment of it had smashed a piece of his heart. After a moment, it occurred to him that these fragments were the shards of his dream. He had rebuilt it before, but now it was crumbled beyond recognition or repair.

There was anguish in his voice when he spoke; anguish over the destruction of his dream, but anguish for young Hepburn too. Anguish and the growing of a terrible, frightening wrath.

"Did Kyle kill the kid? What the hell would he do that for?"

"I don't know who killed him," said Lane, sweat streaming down his lean cheeks, eyes sad and wild. "All I know is that he was found dead and you've been blamed for it. And all because of Kyle."

"What'd he do?"

Lane sucked in his breath and it made a soft wail. "Kyle told all about you, Steve." Something constricted about Britton's neck like the tightening of the hangman's noose. "He told about you having been in the pen for rustling. I don't know if he said anymore, but that was enough. When Bob was found dead, Rambone said right off that you'd killed him. He said you've been rustling Chain Link cattle and Bob found out and that's why you killed him, so he couldn't tell."

Britton sat there in the saddle, stunned. For the moment, his mind refused to function. He told himself that this was the irresponsible, confused rambling of a nightmare out of which he would waken soon. It was that unreal to him at first.

Lane uttered that helpless, wrathful sob again. "That goddam Kyle. If he hadn't told about you, you wouldn't have got the blame. Frank Hepburn sent a wire to Las Cruces and when the answer came back he put a price on your head. Dead or alive, Steve! That's why you've got to get out of the Ladrones. If they catch you, you'll never see a jail or a trial. They'll hang you on the spot!"

"If I run," said Britton, lips moving stiffly, his voice so thick and hoarse it sounded like that of a stranger in his ears, "I'll admit I really killed the kid. I'll never make anybody believe the truth then."

"If you don't run and they catch you, they'll hang you," cried Lane. "Don't you see? Chain Link's riders are searching the Ladrones. Hepburn isn't going to turn you over to the sheriff if he catches you, Steve. You can argue with Hepburn all you want, but will he believe you? Tell me that. Will Hepburn believe you when you say you didn't kill his son?"

Britton balled a fist and smashed it down on the saddle horn. He smashed it again and again in an outburst of helpless fury. He began swearing in a strangled, sobbing, irate way.

Lane turned in his kack and studied the country behind him. He started as he spied something. "Steve!" he cried. "Look. That dust. That'll be Chain Link. You've got to ride, Steve!"

"I won't go," said Britton. His eyes had picked up the faint swirling of dust beyond a rise. The riders, however, were not yet visible. "I'll never clear myself if I run. I ain't gonna be a hunted man the rest of my life."

"That's better than swinging from a tree, isn't it?" cried the boy. He crowded the sorrel in against the black and put his pleading face close to Britton's. "Can't you understand, Steve? Hepburn is crazy mad. You can't reason with him. He wants vengeance for his son. He wants you dead!"

Britton sat there, staring at the dust, rising ever nearer. For a moment despair gripped him and set him to thinking that he might as well be dead now that the dream was gone for good.

"Steve," Lane pleaded. "Snap out of it, Steve. You can outrun them if you start now, because their horses will be tired. Get going, Steve!"

The riders topped the rise and sight of them brought Britton up from the depths of inertia and gloom. There were half a dozen horsemen and when they spied Lane and Britton some of them fired their guns, but the range was too great. However, they were closing in fast.

"Dammit, Steve, move!" screamed the boy. He was sobbing with impotent rage. He crowded his sorrel some more, forcing the black around so that it faced back into the canyon. Britton turned his head and from over his shoulder watched the riders come.

Lane swore and jabbed a spur hard into the black's flank. The horse snorted with pain and jumped ahead. Suddenly, despair and indecision were gone from Britton. He urged the black into a run, but when he looked back he saw that Lane was not following. The boy had dismounted and was running behind several large boulders that littered the mouth of the canyon.

Britton rode back. "What do you think you're doing?" he shouted. "Come on, Eddie."

Lane had his rifle. He aimed it over the top of a boulder and fired. The slug kicked up dust in front of the horsemen and they reined in sharply. Lane fired again and the riders wheeled their mounts and rode off a little way.

Lane looked over his shoulder at Britton, still on the black. "I'll cover for you, Steve. I can hold them off until you get a head start."

"You crazy fool," cried Britton. "Get on your horse. You're coming with me."

"I can hold them off easy. They'll never get into this canyon as long as I've got ammunition."

Fear and the urgency of the moment had worked into the black. It was skittering around, snorting nervously. Britton had to rein it in with an iron grip.

"And when your ammunition gives out, what then?"

"I'll just surrender. It's not me they want. I'm in the clear. Don't you see, Steve? It's you Chain Link wants. You're the only one they want dead. Nothing will happen to me." He gave a reckless laugh. "Oh, they'll be sore as hell at me, but that'll be all. Go on, Steve. Stop wasting time."

Britton's throat filled. His eyes stung. "What're you doing this for, Eddie?"

Lane threw Britton a look that said what a foolish question this was to ask. Then Lane grinned and waved a hand. "Be seeing you, partner," he said.

"Sure," said Britton, hardly able to speak past the impediment that had lodged in his throat. "Be seeing you."

He wheeled the black and spurred it. As he raced up the canyon, he heard a flurry of shots. Some time later another flurry came, faint with distance. After that, there was silence except for the frantic hurrying of the black's hoofs. . . .

12

Britton had a glimpse of three riders late that afternoon. He was on high ground, resting the black in a copse of cedar, and the three passed far below without being at all aware that he was watching. They were too far off for recognition. Nevertheless, Britton had the feeling that they were looking for him. He watched them ride on, toylike and harmless at that distance. His heart was beating with loud, measured strokes.

He crossed a ridge and rode into a stand of timber. The sun was down now. In the trees the shadows thickened quickly. The wind moaned in the tops of the pines, a soft, sad requiem for the beautiful dream that was no more. He rode on until he came to where a bluff reared among the timber. A tiny creek meandered nearby and he reined in the black and prepared to spend the night.

He had no bedroll, only his saddle blanket. He dared not risk a fire for fear that someone might be watching from the heights of a peak towering close by. The only food he had was some jerky he had stuffed in his pocket that morning. He hunkered up close to the foot of the bluff and chewed on the dried meat and afterward he wrapped himself in the blanket and tried to sleep.

He slept only in fitful intervals. When morning

came, he felt tired and cold and miserable. The black, however, had rested well. It had drunk and grazed its fill. Britton replenished his canteen. Then he saddled the black and rode on.

He could have ridden deep into the Ladrones that day, but he did not. He circled the country which had seen the brightest moments of his dream. There was something holding him here, something whose nature he could not define although he did understand that any dallying here could very well result in his death.

He stuck to the timber and the few times he crossed open ground he did so on hard, rocky surfaces that left no trace of his passing. Once he caught sight of a band of horsemen and watched them ride by not half a mile away. His heart hammered long after the riders were out of sight.

At midday, he saw three vultures gather and start wheeling and banking against the immensity of the sky. The feeling of portent this time was very strong. It produced a definite chill that shuddered Britton. Then it was gone, but its clammy aftermath still crawled on his back.

His heart was beating quite fast and hard as he sent the black on. Prudence told him to turn and flee, but something stronger than consideration of his own safety was prompting him. He rode on, watching the vultures. A fourth foul bird came and joined the others.

He knew he was in the vicinity of that canyon

where he had fled while Lane had stood off his pursuers. This was dangerous country, he told himself, but he did not turn back. His eyes watched the vultures as though mesmerized.

They wheeled and circled with a patience that seemed endless and unnerving; but then they had all the time in the world for the dead are dead a long time. So they wheeled and banked against the expanse of the sky, their great black wings as still as death.

Britton came to where the pines reared large and tall. The lowest branches on some of these trees were high enough for a horse and rider to pass underneath and it was under one of these pines that Britton found Eddie Lane.

The wind was blowing and the force of it swayed the boy gently back and forth, but there was no need for tenderness for he could feel nothing anymore. His arms were tied behind his back and there was a space of two feet between his boots and the ground. The rope had been thrown over a stout branch and its other end anchored to a nearby tree.

Britton rode up beside Lane and pulled the still body toward him and then he reached up and cut the rope and when Lane fell, Britton grabbed him and guided him so that he rested across the front of the saddle. Then Britton rode away.

For a while he did not care if anyone saw him. He rode until he came to a cut bank with an overhanging lip and at the bottom of this he dropped Lane. Then Britton climbed to the top of the bank and caved dirt down until Lane was covered completely. After that, he gathered stones which he piled over the dirt. Then he tried to remember a snatch of prayer and when he had mumbled that, Britton rode on.

He remained dry-eyed until he camped that night. Again it was a miserable, lonely stopover without a fire and nothing but a last piece of jerky to chew on. The only water available was that in his canteen. He poured some down the black's throat and then he lay down on his back and watched the stirring of the branches above him.

A moon came up and he lay there, staring wide-eyed at the distant twinkling of the stars. He was tired as he had never been before in his life, but he could not sleep. He lay there thinking.

What was that song that Lane used to sing?

"As I walked out in the streets of Laredo,
As I walked out in Laredo one day,
I spied a poor cowboy wrapped up in white
    linen,
Wrapped up in white linen and cold as the
    clay . . ."

Lane and his Mona. It's a funny thing, thought Britton, but I don't even know her last name. I feel like I've known her all my life, but I've never seen her and I don't even know her last name. All I know is that she's called Mona and lives in Palo Pinto, Texas. When this is over, and it will be over, I'll have to ride to Palo Pinto and tell her how Eddie died. So that I could live. That's what I've got to tell her. . . .

" 'It was once in the saddle I used to go
    dashing,
It was once in the saddle I used to go gay.
'Twas first to drinking and then to card
    playing,
Got shot in the breast, I am dying today . . .' "

Mona, he thought, Mona. I wonder if you're still dreaming the dream you and Eddie had? It's no good to dream, Mona. You put too much in a dream and when it breaks you've got nothing in your hands. You've got nothing but tears and regrets. So stop dreaming, Mona, stop dreaming. . . .

" 'Get six jolly cowboys to carry my coffin,
Get six pretty girls to carry my pall;
Put bunches of roses all over my coffin,
Put roses to deaden the clods as they fall . . .' "

I wonder if you'll cry when I tell you, Mona, thought Britton. I suppose you will because you loved him. I loved him too. He was the dearest friend I had. He was just a plain, hard-working kid with a dream and I loved him. You'll cry, Mona, and I'll cry with you. Just like I'm crying now. . . .

Britton lay on the rock, watching the rider coming up from below. The sun rested warm and pleasant on his back and at times he almost drowsed, but this was as much from hunger as from torpor. Behind him, a ragged peak reared. Below him stretched the panorama of a mountainside.

The rider disappeared into a small stand of cedar, but after a while he emerged. He skirted several windfalls that lay gray and dead on the slope and then veered to the left. He passed close enough below for Britton to make the horse out as a golden palomino.

Britton's heart gave a leap, then quieted. Stella, he told himself, that was Stella Hepburn passing below. But he did not move. He did not cry out. Suspicion roiled uglily in him. His eyes narrowed still more as he scanned the country through which she had come. He watched until his eyes ached, but no one rode in her wake.

Still, he was not entirely trustful. He had had such a bitter taste of deceit that he doubted whether he could ever again accept anything in good faith. The world was rotten. The people in it reeked with the stench of corruption.

He looked for the girl, but she had ridden out of

sight. Heart racing a little, he climbed down from the rock and mounted the black which was now rested. He threw one more cautious look down the mountainside and then started the horse.

Britton picked up the palomino's tracks quickly and he sent the black in pursuit. An uneasy presentiment settled over him and he cast frequent glances over his shoulder, but the land remained lonely and empty.

Finally, he spotted the girl ahead, but he did not overtake her directly. He sent the black up a slope and into some timber and then he rode swiftly through the trees until he estimated he had passed the girl whose palomino was moving at a walk. He rode down the slope and at the edge of the timber, which the girl was skirting, he reined in the black and waited.

She rode around a high boulder almost directly into him and the suddenness was so startling to her that she pulled up with a small scream. Her hand flew up to her open mouth and her widened eyes stared at him with alarm and fear. Then the shock passed. Color rushed back into her face and she spurred the palomino over beside him.

"Steve," she cried. "I'm so glad I found you, Steve."

He had not stirred. He was slouched forward in the saddle, shoulders sagging, hands crossed on the horn. The black beard and the thin, tight line of his mouth and the brooding eyes with the agate hardness in them lent a sinistrous, forbidding cast to his features. The girl seemed taken aback by this. She had started to reach out a hand toward him, but now she withdrew it. She edged the palomino away a little.

"What're you doing here?" he asked. His voice was a growl.

"I've been looking for you, Steve," she said in a subdued tone scarcely above a whisper. Her eyes flicked fearfully over him. "I've been looking for you for three days."

"Why?"

"I want to help you."

The sound he emitted was meant to be a laugh of disdain, but it was more of a ferine snarl. The girl flinched when she heard it. Her eyes misted and then dropped. After a while, she found some courage and her head lifted.

"I stopped by your camp and got some things for you," she said, hipping around in the saddle. "I've got your bedroll and some grub and ammunition. I—I figured you'd be needing them."

Shame began to creep into Britton, but the dark suspicion still lingered. "They say I killed your brother," he said. "They'll hang me for it if they catch me. Yet you say you want to help me. Why?"

The girl's head came up sharply as she laid a surprised look on him. "I know what they say, but I also know it isn't true."

"I'm an ex-convict. Don't you believe that?"

She nodded.

"Doesn't it follow then that I killed your brother?"

"Oh, Steve, Steve," she cried, reining the palomino in close and reaching out to take him by the arms. "Why are you so bitter, Steve? I don't care what anyone else believes. I know you didn't kill Bob. From the very beginning I knew it wasn't you. Why do you think I rode out to warn you? Why do you think I've been riding the Ladrones trying to find you? What reason would you have for killing Bob? You were the best friend he had. He worshiped you, Steve, you don't know how he worshiped you. You went out of your way to help him. Why would you kill him?"

With her head dropped back and her face there close to him, he could see the shadows fatigue had put under her eyes and the tiny lines about the corners of her mouth and the way her cheeks had started to gaunt. Her eyes were luminous with hurt, a hurt that was more than sorrow and grief for her dead brother. Some of that hurt was there because of him, Steve Britton, ex-convict and rustler.

The feeling that came over him then caused his throat to fill so that he could not speak. His eyes began to sting and he dropped his head in remorse and shame for what he had thought and said. She put her arms around him and he drew her close, hungrily and crushingly. He buried his face against the golden silk of her hair. Several tears fell there but she never knew it. . . .

The girl sat and watched Britton eat. He wolfed the food down, gulping loudly. When he was through, he leaned back, resting himself against the bole of a pine. He rolled a cigarette and smoked.

He watched the girl sitting there, legs tucked under her. The buckskin riding skirt was soiled, the red flannel jacket's brightness was dimmed by a faint coating of dust. She sat in an attitude that suggested great weariness. The lines about her mouth gave her an almost haggard look.

He could feel his heart beating with quick, strong strokes. He was thinking that he was not alone anymore. He had her in his hour of adversity and there was no one he would rather have. But this was no good. For her it was no good.

"You'll have to go, Stella," he said gently.

Her head came up. Shock widened her eyes. "Steve?"

He made a gesture as if that would explain what he meant, but it did not and he knew he had to put it into words. He searched for them.

"You can't stay, Stella," he said slowly. "I don't know what's going to happen to me. They're all over the Ladrones looking for me. I might shake them and then again I might not. I—I don't want you around if they should catch me. It won't be nice, Stella."

Her eyes were bright as though on the brink of panic. "Aren't you leaving the Ladrones?" she asked.

Britton shook his head.

"But why?"

He did not answer this. He straightened and rose to his feet. He stared down at her awhile, dark and poignant thoughts churning around in his mind. Then he went over to her palomino and tightened the cinches.

"You'll probably run into some Chain Link riders," he said. "One of them will take you home."

She came slowly upright. A moment she stared at him in unbelief. Then she started toward him with awkward, hesitant steps. She stopped in front of him and her fingers twined.

"I won't go, Steve," she said, lips moving stiffly.

Something stuck in his throat and it made him angry. "Look, Stella," he said with some exasperation, "you know what Chain Link wants me for. It won't be pretty once they catch me. Do I have to say more? Now get on your horse and go."

Her face grew old as she thought on something. But a grim purpose glinted in her eyes and hardened the lines of her features. "I'll never go," she whispered. "I'll never leave you. You need me now and I won't leave you. I can help you, Steve. Don't you see? You can hold me as a hostage. Chain Link won't dare harm you as long as you've got me as a hostage."

He shook his head stubbornly. "I don't want anything to happen to you. You stick with me and you might get hurt too."

"Would that be bad?" she said. "If something happens to you, I don't want to go on anymore. Without you there wouldn't be anything for me. If something is going to happen to you, I want it to happen to me too."

His eyes filled suddenly and he looked away so that she might not see. He stared awhile at the naked top of a peak, overwhelmed by a sensation he had never experienced before. He was aware that she was studying him intently, but he kept his face averted.

After a while, she asked, "Why won't you leave the Ladrones?"

He took his eyes off the peak and stared at the ground. They were dry now and hard. He said nothing.

"Do you want to square for Bob?"

"Something like that."

"It isn't worth losing your life," she said.

"It isn't only Bob. There's Eddie, too."

He heard her sharp gasp. "Eddie?"

A savage burst of wrath surged across his mind.

"Yes, Eddie," he snarled. "He's dead too. Both of those kids are dead and all because someone hates me."

"But—but how did it happen with Eddie?"

He turned and stared at her narrowly. It dawned on him that she did not know or understand. "I found Eddie hanging from a pine," he said slowly, anguish wrenching his heart. Remembrance of the moment brought beads of sweat out on his brow. "I don't know who did it, but I can guess. Chain Link hanged him."

Horror twisted the girl's face. Her lips moved soundlessly awhile before any words came. "But why? Why Eddie?"

"Because he warned me and helped me get away. I didn't think Chain Link"—he almost said "your father"—"could hate that way. Eddie thought and I thought they'd rough him up a bit, but that wasn't enough for Chain Link. They hanged him."

The girl started to cry. Her head dropped and she pressed her palms against her face and the sobs came hoarsely and brokenly. Britton watched her. There were no tears in him. All the tears he would ever shed had been spilled the night before. All that remained in him was a purpose and a hate. A vile, malevolent, relentless purpose.

His glance lifted and he stared bleakly off into a world where there was only brutality and death. "I've never killed a man," he said, "and

I never thought I would, but I am going to kill now. I don't know exactly who or how many, but I am going to kill. Even if it means the end of every-thing, I am still going to kill. I'll kill if it's the last thing I do—"

13

They reined in their horses and dismounted while the animals rested. Britton dropped to the ground and crawled on his belly to the rim of a ledge that gave him a good view of the mountainside below. Down there he spied three horsemen.

He studied them a long time. He was aware of Stella edging up beside him, but he did not glance at her. With a grim preoccupation, he went on watching. He could hear the hard, uniform pulsing of his heart against the stone.

The riders crossed an open stretch of ground and entered a stand of timber. Though they were gone from sight, Britton knew where they would emerge for they were following his tracks. He waited patiently, eyes fixed on the spot. The girl reached over once and laid a hand lightly on his arm, but Britton did not stir nor look at her. A deep and malevolent wrath was building up in him.

He had a vision once of Eddie Lane swinging slowly in the wind and Britton shut his eyes to wipe the memory from his mind. Anguish wrenched his heart, then was gone, and only the hate and the brutal purpose remained. When he opened his eyes, he saw the riders coming out of the trees.

They were visible only briefly. Then they were in the timber again, doubling back as Britton's tracks had done. Britton edged back from the rim and rose to his feet. He went over and pulled his Winchester from the saddle boot and checked the loads. Then he tightened the black's cinches. When he turned, he found the girl watching him, eyes wide with concern and fear.

"I'll be gone awhile, Stella," he said quietly. "You wait here."

Her lips paled as she studied the stern lines of his face. The black beard stubble heightened the cruel glint in his eyes. The thin, taut shape of his mouth attested to the brutal impulse which had seized him.

"Where are you going?" she asked.

"Down below."

She knew what he meant and what he intended. The concern deepened in her eyes, leaving them sad and forlorn. The skin tightened over the crests of her cheeks. She made no effort to stop him though it was apparent she did not want him to go.

"Who are they?" she asked.

"Mingo and his pals."

"Mingo?"

He realized she had no way of knowing who or what Mingo was and Britton had no desire to tell her. He said, "There's a price on my head. It'll be paid to anyone who brings me in. There's more than Chain Link after me."

Mention of Chain Link hurt her. Her head dropped and her shoulders sagged and she looked as though she were going to cry, but not a sound escaped her. Seeing her like that filled Britton with a great compassion, so that for an instant the hate and the purpose were forgotten.

He put his hands on her shoulders, but she would not lift her head. "I've got to go, Stella," he said gently. "Can't you see? It's my best chance. They've picked up my trail and they'll keep after it until they catch up with me. My best play is to go down to them. I'll have the advantage that way because I'll know just where they'll be passing. It's either me or them, Stella."

She nodded without raising her head. She uttered no sound. Britton bent his head and kissed her tenderly on the cheek. The instant his lips touched her she shuddered as if in the grip of a great convulsion. Then she was still again.

Britton mounted. When he reined the black around, the girl raised her head, turning her face up to him, and he read the urgent appeal on her distraught features and the pain and the prayer in her moistened eyes. He was going to speak but something filled his throat, stifling all sound. So he smiled a little and raised a hand slightly in a gesture of farewell.

The black started at the soft touch of Britton's spurs. . . .

• • •

He rode down the mountainside, saddened and lonely at first. As the black passed into a grove of junipers, Britton was thinking that he had had a taste of his dream. Not much, just the barest taste, and it was not enough. He wanted a lifetime to cherish and nurture the dream, but the way the cards were stacked he might never know its touch again.

Thinking thus brought the wrath and the hate back. Memory of the girl and the dream faded in him. Soon his mind held nothing but the brutal intent. He rode on with slitted, wrath-bright eyes, keeping to the shelter of the timber all the while, going ever downward to a point he had fixed in his mind.

He had it figured that Mingo and Surratt and Gerber would not reach that spot ahead of him, even though he would cover the last part of it on foot. He halted the black and stepped down and then tied the lines to a juniper. Taking the Winchester, he slithered down an incline that momentarily left him revealed in the harsh light of the sun. Then he was down among some bushes and crawling along on his hands and knees until he came to where this crag of rock terminated abruptly. At the foot of the crag he could see the tracks laid down by his black and the palomino.

He hunkered down at the edge of the crag behind a large sliver of stone that thrust up enough to partially conceal him. He made sure that there was a shell in the breech of the Winchester and then he settled down to wait.

The minutes dragged on, seeming as interminable and infinite as the passing of an eon. Sweat came out on the palms of his hands and wetted the rifle where he gripped it. The sun bore straight down, casting only the tiniest shadows. Its intensity was as merciless as the feeling in his heart.

Sweat beaded his brow and dampened the whiskers on his cheeks and above his mouth before he caught the first hint of a sound. It was so slight that at first he thought it was just his imagination and he went on listening, straining for the repetition which did not seem to be coming.

He had just started to relax, thinking that his ears had tricked him, when it sounded again and this time there was no doubt as to its reality. What Britton heard was the sharp ring of a shod hoof against stone.

He tensed and the Winchester rose. The butt nestled against his shoulder and he looked down the long barrel to where the three would come riding out of the trees. His thumb cocked the hammer. Then he crouched there, motionless, listening and waiting.

He picked up the faint squeal of saddle leather and then the soft snort of a horse and after that the murmur of a voice. In Britton's ears his own heart pounded as loud as a drum. He swallowed and his throat was so dry and stiff that the movement produced a sharp pain.

The horse snorted again and then emerged into the open. Gerber was leading the way, scanning the country ahead with narrowed eyes and mouth parted in the effort of concentration. Sun glinted off the barrel of the Winchester in Britton's hands and this warned Gerber.

He cried out even as his glance flashed up. He was just reaching for his gun when Britton fired. The slug smashed down through the top of Gerber's skull, snuffing the life out of him instantly. He started to fold over gently in the saddle, but his horse gave a sudden, frightened lurch and this dislodged Gerber and he tumbled out of the kack.

The horse wheeled completely around, smashing into both Surratt's and Mingo's mounts. Surratt had been carrying a carbine in his right hand and he had the gun almost to his shoulder when Gerber's panicked horse hit his own bay. The impact was so strong that it rocked Surratt in his seat. He fired, but the barrel of the carbine had tilted upward and the bullet shrieked up the mountainside.

Britton's slug took Surratt in the chest. He groaned with intense hurt and came straining up in the stirrups, the carbine falling from his hands. Panic had gripped his bay also. The animal squealed with fright and shied, colliding with Mingo's dun. The shock of this sent Surratt lunging to the side. He made a grab for his saddle horn, but his fingers missed and then he was going out of the saddle, dropping down between his own bay and Gerber's chestnut. The chestnut screamed with terror and kicked out and one of the hoofs caught Surratt on the back of the neck and snapped it. His bay stumbled as it rebounded off Mingo's dun and came crashing down on Surratt, but he never felt it. He was beyond feeling anything anymore.

In the tangle of panicked, squealing, milling horses, Mingo cursed savagely. He could see Britton up above, aiming the Winchester at him. Britton fired, but the dun lunged sideways at the same time and Britton missed. Because Mingo needed one hand to check the terror-stricken dun, he used his six-shooter. The shot he snapped up at Britton chipped a sliver of stone off the rock next to Britton's cheek.

Swiftly, Britton levered another shell into the breech and this time he caught Mingo's chest in the sights. As Britton was squeezing the trigger, however, the dun plunged ahead. The bullet caught Mingo in the shoulder and the pain and the impact twisted him halfway around in the saddle. Surratt's bay in rising came up under the dun's neck and the dun reared high. Mingo went sailing over the cantle of his saddle, six-shooter falling from his hand. He hit the ground on his bad shoulder and shrieked with pain. He rolled over convulsively on his stomach and lay there, breathing hard and moaning.

Holding his Winchester in his left hand and his .44 in his right, Britton came sliding down the side of the crag. The sleeve of his jacket caught on a protruding jag and ripped up to the elbow, but he paid it no heed. His eyes were fixed on Mingo, still moaning on the ground. Gerber and Surratt were both dead and needed no watching.

The violence had heightened rather than abated the wrath and the hate in Britton. He was almost sobbing from the virulence of the emotions that racked him. A searing vision of Eddie Lane swinging from the pine nearly blinded Britton. There was no pity or compassion in him as he stood over Mingo.

With the toe of his boot he jabbed Mingo in the ribs. The man groaned, but did not stir. In a vicious burst of rage, Britton got his boot under the man's side and rolled him over with a roughness that tore a cry out of Mingo. He lay on his back, large, glassy eyes bright with a venomous hate as they glared up at Britton.

"Who killed young Hepburn, Mingo?" growled Britton.

"I'm hurt," moaned Mingo, breathing hard.

"You're not hurt that bad," said Britton, peering at Mingo's blood-soaked shoulder. "Get up."

"I'm hurt," Mingo moaned again.

"You can at least sit up," snarled Britton. He

poised his boot. "Do you want *me* to get you up?"

Mingo shook his head. He got his good elbow under him and pushed himself up to a sitting position. He sat there, chest heaving, making small, sniveling sounds.

"You can stop crying," Britton said brutally, "because that won't buy you anything, Mingo. There's just one thing that will make me go easy on you. Tell me who killed young Hepburn. Was it Rambone?"

Slowly, Mingo raised his head. The skin seemed to be drawn tighter than ever over the prominent bones of his face, drawn almost to the cracking point. The large eyes were no longer indifferent or inscrutable. They glowed with a crafty and profound thoughtfulness. Awhile Mingo stared up like that. His moaning ceased. The rise and fall of his breast became even and normal.

"Damn you," said Mingo.

Britton's grip on his six-shooter tightened to the extent that his knuckles turned white. He had to swallow a deep breath to contain himself. His lips grew dry and stiff with wrath.

"You'd better tell me, Mingo."

Mingo's eyes narrowed ever so slightly. He paused and appeared to be thinking on something. After a while, he said, "I don't know what you're talking about."

"You know all right," growled Britton. "Why have you been tracking me?"

"Chain Link's put a price of a thousand dollars on your head. Me and the boys figured to take a crack at it."

"Is that the only reason?"

"What do you mean?"

"What's your connection with Rambone?"

"Rambone?" Mingo echoed. "I don't know the man. All I know from hearsay is that he's Chain Link's ramrod."

"You're a goddam liar, Mingo."

Resentment darkened Mingo's face. Then he caught himself. He shifted his position slightly and the bland, inscrutable expression came over his features.

"You won't get a rise out of me like that, Britton."

Rage was running hot and violent in Britton's blood. He kept getting visions of Lane hanging from a tree and the images tormented and infuriated him. He tried to suppress the memory for he did not want to be carried away by it. He had no idea what extremes he would resort to if he got carried away.

He took a deep breath. "There's some connection between you and Rambone," he said, voice thick from the control he was imposing on himself. "I don't know exactly what it is, but you're going to tell me. Rambone hates my guts. I'm beginning to suspect why. He wants me out of the way. He wants me dead. Is that why you tried to egg me into a gunfight that day at the camp? Did Rambone send you to kill me?"

"You're crazy. You riled me that day, Britton. You riled me and my boys. We weren't going to take that kind of crap from you or anyone else. If it had come to shooting, you had no one to blame but yourself."

"I still say Rambone sent you."

Long, deep wrinkles creased Mingo's cheeks as he sneered. "If Rambone had hired me to kill you, I could have done it many times easy."

"As easy as that day in the canyon?" said Britton. A thought struck him. "What're you hiding up that canyon, Mingo? Chain Link cattle?"

Mingo laughed derisively. "Now that makes sense," he jeered. "First you accuse me of being in cahoots with Rambone. Then you accuse me of stealing Chain Link beef. What more proof do you want that you're off your rocker, Britton?"

"All right," snarled Britton, angry and impatient. "We'll go back to who killed Bob Hepburn. Was it Rambone?"

"How should I know?"

"Maybe it was you, Mingo. Was it?"

Mingo's eyes brightened as if in mocking amusement. "Damn you," he said.

The rage that seized Britton now blinded him to everything else. Snarling and half sobbing, he braced a boot against Mingo's good shoulder and with a vicious shove spun the man so that he flopped on his stomach. Mingo cried out in pain and alarm, but before he could begin to rise Britton was on him, pinning him down with a knee rammed against the small of his back. Mingo squirmed and twisted, but Britton grabbed the man's arms and jerked them behind his back. He ripped the bandanna from around Mingo's neck and tied his wrists together. Then Britton rose to his feet, wrath and exertion making his breath come fast and hot.

Mingo's dun had come to a stop nearby when it had started stepping on the lines. Britton went over to the horse and mounted. He took the rope off the saddle and shook out a small loop and sent the dun over to Mingo who had scrambled with panting effort to his feet. Mingo's eyes widened with fear when he saw Britton ride at him and Mingo turned to flee. His bound arms hampered him and Britton rode up beside Mingo and dropped the loop around Mingo's neck. He started to cry out, but then the noose tightened and Mingo's shout ended in a strangling gurgle.

Britton's mind held only hate and brutality. Every other sensitivity that he might ever have possessed was completely forgotten. Pain and suffering no longer moved him. His heart at this moment was as unfeeling as a fragment of stone.

He tossed the end of the lariat over the branch of a tree and made a dally around the saddle horn and started backing the dun. Mingo went along until he was directly under the limb. There the rope tightened and Mingo could move no more. Britton backed the dun until Mingo's toes strained to touch the ground.

"How do you like it, Mingo?" shouted Britton, his cries echoing through the avenues of the trees. "This is how Eddie died, but he died quick. I won't hang you that way, Mingo. I'll hang you slow. That's no more than fair, isn't it? Eddie had no part in this. He was just a kid with a dream, but they hanged him anyway because he was my friend and did me a good turn." His voice broke, but only an instant, then the rage was back in it again, bestial and unrelenting. "Eddie died because of Rambone's scheming and you were a part of that scheming and so you'll die, too, Mingo. There's only one thing can save you. Tell me who killed young Hepburn. If you won't or can't, you'll die."

Mingo's head was racked to one side, the cords standing out in his neck as he strained to get the tiniest bit of slack in the rope. His mouth gaped and worked spasmodically, his eyes bulged, but only guttural gasps and exhalations emerged. His face started to purple before Britton moved the dun ahead enough for Mingo to get both heels back on the ground.

Britton's voice was hard and cruel. "This is your last chance, Mingo. If you think I'm bluffing, you don't have to tell me anything. That way we'll both find out if I'll go through with this."

Mingo drew in air with great, whistling gulps. He teetered on his feet and once it looked as though he were going to sag, but when his knees gave way a little the noose bit into his neck and this brought Mingo upright and tense once more. He sucked in another breath and it made a sound like a sob.

"All right, Britton, all right," he panted. "Let me down and I'll tell you everything."

"You'll tell me first," said Britton. "You'll tell me everything I want to know before I put anymore slack in this rope. Start with young Hepburn."

Mingo was drawing prodigious breaths and they hampered his speech, but still he managed to get the words out in a labored, moaning way. "Rambone killed the kid."

"You aren't lying?"

"No, Britton. I swear I'm not. Rambone killed him."

"Why?"

"He wants Chain Link."

"How would that get him Chain Link?"

Mingo swallowed and the effort ripped a small groan out of him. "He figures on marrying the Hepburn girl. With the kid out of the way, Rambone will have all of Chain Link when old Hepburn dies."

"All right," said Britton, voice still cold and grim. "Who's in it with Rambone?"

"Let me down, Britton," Mingo pleaded. "God, I can hardly breathe. Please let me down."

"I'll let you down when you're through. Tell me now. Who else is in it with Rambone?"

"There's only him."

"I won't have you lying to me, Mingo!"

Mingo's voice grew shrill with pain and desperation. "I swear to God I'm not lying. Please believe me, Britton. There's no one but Rambone."

"What about you? Aren't you part of it?"

"Not all of it," moaned Mingo. "I had nothing to do with killing the kid. That was all Rambone's idea."

"What part were you in?"

"Rambone was out to get you from the first. He saw the Hepburn girl falling for you and he didn't want anybody taking her from him. He had no idea who you were other than a greasy-sack mustanger and he decided to frame you. He hired me and the boys to rustle some Chain Link cattle. That's what we've got up that canyon. He was going to blame you for that. When he found out about your prison record, he decided to go all the way. He killed the kid then with the idea of pinning that on you and getting Chain Link all to himself. But I had nothing to do with the kid. I was in on the rustling but that is all."

"Why were you tracking me? You meant to kill me, didn't you?"

"Rambone sent us out," gasped Mingo, sweat storming down his cheeks. "Chain Link's riders are split in two bunches, one under Rambone, the other under Hepburn. Rambone told us there would be another thousand in it for us if we made sure you couldn't talk. You can't blame me for that, Britton. Rambone has me over a barrel. If I don't go along with him, he can always get me for running off those Chain Link cows."

"What about Reeve?"

"Reeve?"

"Yes—Reeve. Kyle Reeve," snarled Britton. "My partner. Isn't he in this with Rambone?"

"Not that I know of. All Reeve did was to tell Rambone that you were in the pen for rustling. Rambone did the rest."

"You aren't lying to me, Mingo?"

"Oh, God, no!" screamed Mingo.

"You'll tell Chain Link this? You'll tell them just like you've told me?"

Mingo was crying. "Anything you want, Britton, anything. Only please let me down. I can't stand this no more. Please let me down—"

14

They headed west, toward Chain Link, with Mingo reeling a little in the saddle. He was not seriously hurt, but he had lost a lot of blood. Britton had fixed a crude bandage about the wound and the bleeding had stopped. Despite Mingo's condition, Britton was taking no chances. He had tied Mingo's ankles together under the belly of the dun. Britton led the horse. Stella Hepburn rode beside him.

Once Britton thought he spied something, a flicker of movement on a ridge to his left, but when he hipped around in the saddle and threw a look up there the trace was gone. He had no idea what it had been. He was not even sure that there had been anything. A faint uneasiness settled between his shoulder blades.

The girl kept casting looks at him. He was aware of the worry in her glances for the lines of his face were still hard and stern. He tried reassuring her with a smile now and then, but each attempt was an effort and never quite came off because the rage and the hate still roiled in him.

Along toward sundown as they were crossing a small, barren plain, a group of riders burst over a rise and when they spied Britton and Mingo and the girl the horsemen spurred their mounts into a

223

gallop. They thundered across the plain, raising a great, billowing cloud of dust.

Britton reined in his black, his heart growing cold and angry. With narrowed, hate-ridden eyes he watched the riders come. The girl had cried out softly in alarm and fright when she recognized the horsemen as Chain Link. She edged the palomino over next to Britton and leaned toward him as though wanting to shield him. He put a hand tenderly on her arm and smiled briefly. His eyes, however, remained angry and grim.

He turned once in the saddle and told Mingo, "Tell it like you told it to me and to Miss Hepburn. You tell it any different, Mingo, and, so help me, I'll kill you."

Mingo said nothing. The indifference and blandness, however, were absent from his features. His gaunt cheeks were ashen, the skin along his jaw was so taut that the bone shone white underneath.

Chain Link reined in amid a spuming, churning cloud of dust. One of the horses coughed and then for a while there was only silence except for the fretful stirring of some of the animals and their hard breathing. The faces of the men seen through the dust were stern and forbidding.

The grayness on Frank Hepburn's features was not all dust. Pain was there and through the agate hardness of his eyes could be seen the tortured feeling of irrevocable loss. He had ridden up with his six-shooter in his hand and now he started raising the gun slowly.

The girl saw and cried out. "No," she screamed, spurring the palomino and jumping it so that she was between Britton and her father. "No. He didn't kill Bob. Rambone killed him. Rambone. Ask Mingo. Rambone killed Bob."

"Get out of the way, Stella," said Hepburn. He evinced no indication that he had heard or understood her words. Madness mingled with the pain in his eyes. "Get out of the way."

"No," the girl cried. "Not until you've heard Mingo. Steve wouldn't kill Bob. Why, Steve was the best friend Bob had. Steve liked Bob and Bob worshiped him. He loved Steve as much as he hated you!"

The shock of this stiffened Hepburn perceptibly. His face paled still more. All at once the hardness vanished completely from his eyes. They brightened almost to the point of tears with a luminosity of anguish and regret. A moment he was like this, staring out at something that only he could see. The gun lowered in his hand until the barrel rested against his thigh. Then the focus of his eyes returned to the present. The hardness began to glint in them again.

"Rambone?" said Hepburn, his voice revealing no sign of the turmoil that was raging inside him. "Why would Rambone want to kill my son? He works for Chain Link. Why would *he* kill my boy?"

Words failed the girl. Her head dropped and a sob shook her. Britton turned in the saddle and threw a look at Mingo.

"Tell him, Mingo," said Britton.

Mingo swallowed and the effort seemed to remind him of the rope that had been so tight around his neck for he lifted a hand and gently touched his throat.

"Tell him," Britton said again, voice frigid.

There was a haunted, fear-filled quality in the glassy brightness of Mingo's glance. "Rambone wants Chain Link," he said.

"How will that ever get him Chain Link?" snapped Hepburn.

"He was fixing to marry your girl and he would get Chain Link through her when you died. He didn't want to share it with your kid."

Hepburn's face twitched once as if he had been gripped by an agonized spasm. Wrath was building up in him. He finally took his eyes off Britton and fixed the hard, irate glance on Mingo.

"You saw Rambone kill my boy?" he growled. "You were there?"

"No, no," cried Mingo, a sudden rush of terror making his voice shrill. "Rambone didn't tell me a thing until after it was over. He left me behind while he rode into the kid's camp. I heard a shot and then Rambone came out and told me to give him a hand to lift the kid on a horse. He didn't tell me until then that he figured on framing the killing on Britton. I had no idea at all that he was going to kill your kid, Hepburn."

"Still you were there," growled Hepburn, something implacable entering his tone. "You were in with Rambone all the while."

"Only for framing Britton," cried Mingo, eyes watching the bared gun in Hepburn's hand as though mesmerized. "Rambone wanted Britton out of the Ladrones. He got me to run off some Chain Link cows and then he was going to frame it on Britton. That's the only part I was in, Hepburn. I had nothing to do with your kid. I swear I didn't."

Hepburn's face twitched again. Something cruel and merciless glinted in his eyes. The gun in his hand started to rise and his teeth bared when he spoke.

"You were there when my boy was killed," he snarled. "You were there."

Britton saw the ugly, brutal intent on Hepburn's face and so did Mingo. Mingo shouted in fear and terror and threw up his hands as though they could ward off the bullets. Britton spurred the black, jumping it ahead so that it crowded hard against Hepburn's orange dun. Britton grabbed Hepburn's wrist and pushed it down.

Anger and resentment darkened Hepburn's face. He strove to free his wrist, lurching sideways in the saddle, the cords standing out in his neck, but Britton stayed with him.

"Mingo had nothing to do with the death of your son," cried Britton. "I believe the man when he says that. You can't kill him for running off your cows. It'll be murder, Hepburn."

Rage and hate and anguish had maddened Hepburn. His eyes glowered, his lips curled back from his teeth and his face twitched spasmodically.

"He was in with Rambone and Rambone killed my son. He'll die for that. He helped to kill my son!"

"And you helped to kill my partner!"

The insufferableness of it erupted in Britton in a rush of anguish and hate. He felt his whole being caught up in this vortex of savagery. His chest swelled with it, his brain ached with it. He was half sobbing as he spoke.

"He was a kid, too, a little older than your boy," cried Britton, crowding the black against the dun with an insistence that forced the dun to back a little. Britton's face was thrust out; his fingers dug into Hepburn's wrist with such a fury that Hepburn's grip loosened and the six-shooter fell to the ground. "He was a good, hard worker and he never hurt anyone in his life and you strung him up because he helped me. He was just a kid with a dream and a girl waiting for him back in Texas. Who's going to tell that girl Eddie's dead? Will you go to Palo Pinto and tell her, Hepburn?

"If there is any killing to be done around here, I'm the one who should be doing it. You're the one who should die. But as much as I hate your guts and as much as you need it, I won't kill you. There's just two more men I'm going to kill and you aren't one of them."

Hate and anguish and regret were running in Britton like a current. "I suppose you'll cry for the son you drove from you, Hepburn, and when you do save some tears for Eddie Lane and his Mona. Cry for them too. Cry for them if there is anything decent and good left in that rotten, stinking heart of yours—"

When the Chain Link riders, led by a subdued and remorseful old man, left with Mingo, Stella Hepburn would not go with them. She sat on her palomino beside Britton, watching the cavalcade ride away.

There was sadness in Britton as he observed the tight, determined cast of her features. "Go to him, Stella," he said after a while. "He needs you."

"I'll never go back to Chain Link," she said. "He's the one who put those ideas in Rambone's head. I never wanted to marry Rambone, but he would have forced me to. Because Rambone was sure of this, he killed Bob." She shook her head. "I'll never set foot on Chain Link again."

"He's all alone now, Stella," Britton said gently. "If he doesn't have you, then he has nothing. Go to him. You'll never regret it."

She turned her head and stared up at him. Wonder and puzzlement wrinkled her brow and narrowed her eyes. She was looking at him as though she were seeing a new and startling side of him.

"What makes you talk like this?" she asked. "I thought you hated him."

"I do," said Britton. His lips tightened. Bleakness entered his eyes and they lifted from her face and stared out into the vast distances. "I'll always hate him for what he did to Eddie, but that can't stop me from feeling sorry for him and being fair to him." He brought his glance back and stared at her urgently. "He's lost a son, Stella. Over the years he'll regret that very much. Don't let him lose you too."

"But I want to stay with you, Steve."

His eyes glinted uglily and he averted his head, but not before she had noticed the look and the hardening of the lines of his face. "You can't be with me for a while yet, Stella."

Her whisper was barely audible. "Don't you want me?"

"You know it isn't that. I've got a couple of chores to do first. Then I'll send for you."

"You don't have to go after Rambone. Father will take care of that."

"It isn't only Rambone."

"Who else is there?"

He spat the word with a venom and vehemence that made the girl start.

"Reeve!"

• • •

After the girl had gone, the world turned dark and empty for Britton. He rode through the thickening shadows and the stars were twinkling brightly in a clear sky when he reached the canyon that had seen the beginning and the end of his dream.

He rode with saddened heart to the corrals and found the gates open. There wasn't a mustang in the canyon. Chain Link, in wrath and spite, had probably done this. He unsaddled the black and penned it in a corral and then he started back slowly for the camp site, his spurs mourning softly.

He started a fire as he had done so many times and then he sat on his haunches, staring bleakly into the flames, grimly and bitterly considering everything that had passed here in this canyon. He got to thinking that the brightest moments of his life had been, strangely enough, the time he had spent in the penitentiary. That was when the dream had been born and it had been a beautiful, illusory thing then that had sustained him. Now the dream was a shambles. He could have Stella if he wanted her, but too many things had passed, things that took the sweetness and the joy out of having her. As much as he yearned for her, there were other matters he had to attend to. His heart told him this. He had to attend to these matters even if they meant his death and there was a very good chance that death was all he would get out of them.

It was the pangs of hunger that finally aroused him. Nevertheless, he could not find the will to cook himself anything. He made some coffee and drank this while he chewed on dried jerky. Everything seemed tasteless and vapid.

Afterward, he had a cigarette. Then he unrolled his blankets and got in them. He watched the stars shining overhead while he waited for sleep and it seemed that tonight sleep would never come even though he was worn and weary with exhaustion. After a long time, however, he dropped off.

He awoke with the light of the sun bright and searing on his eyes and in his heart a cold, dread feeling that something was amiss. He came up abruptly on an elbow, startled glance searching about him, and he had only to turn his head slightly to the left to look squarely into the black, gaping muzzle of a .45.

Kyle Reeve said, "Easy does it, Steve. We've got your guns so take it easy."

He was sitting on a rock with his shoulders slouched a little and his left arm resting across his thighs. His right arm was crooked and rigid at his side and the .45 in his grip was as motionless as any of the towering peaks of the Ladrones. The bore of the gun looked directly at Britton's heart.

Breath froze an instant in Britton's throat, stifling him. It seemed that for a moment his heart had stilled with the permanence of death, but then it started up again, racing in a hard, raging way. Wrath began to rise, swelling his breast, filling his whole body with a fierce, intolerable pain.

Britton moved his eyes from Reeve and saw Carmen. She stood to one side in a huddled way. When his grim, irate glance raked her, she dropped her eyes and then her head. She kicked once with a toe at the ground. Then she was still. At her feet lay Britton's Winchester and his shell belt and holstered .44.

"I want to talk to you, Steve," said Reeve. "That's why I'm doing it this way. I got the drop on you because I want you to listen to me."

"We've got nothing to talk about," snarled Britton. "Kill me while you've got the chance. Kill me now because if you don't, I'm killing you."

Reeve's shoulders squared as he tensed somewhat. Under the tawny mustache his mouth looked grave and grim. The yellow eyes held a cold, glittering opacity.

"If I had killing in mind, I'd do it without talking," said Reeve. His .45 still pointed at Britton's heart. "But I want you to know how it really was. I could have run and maybe you'd never have found me, but I stayed because I want you to know how it really was. I didn't mean anything against Eddie or the Hepburn kid. I was just sore at you. I knew Rambone hated your guts and he'd jump at the chance to get you out of the Ladrones. I figured that when he found out about you doing time for rustling, he'd frame something on you and you'd go to the pen again.

"That was all right with me because I was sore at you. I never figured Rambone for what he did. I didn't figure on him killing the Hepburn kid and then Eddie getting hung. I didn't figure on anything like that." Sweat had popped out on his brow. Trickles of it coursed crookedly down the shaven planes of his cheeks. "You can't hold me responsible for that, Steve. You can't ask me to answer for that. For what I did to you, yes, but not young Hepburn or Eddie."

Britton's eyes were slitted. They had locked with Reeve's and now they were fixed there, glowing with a wicked, implacable hatred. "How did you find out I was cleared?"

"I've been hanging around Chain Link. I was there when Mingo was brought in. Rambone's skipped. He spotted you with Mingo and he figured everything was up and he's run for it."

Slowly, Britton threw off his blankets. He pulled his legs in under him and crouched there, eyes glaring steadily at Reeve.

A corner of Reeve's mouth twitched. Several drops of sweat dripped off his chin. "Listen to me, Steve. I know what Eddie meant to you, but you can't hold me accountable for that. He was my partner too."

"He had a dream," growled Britton, thinking that his was not the only dream that had broken, but he was alive and perhaps he could salvage something out of the wreckage, but Lane was dead. Nothing could be salvaged there. Only a memory remained and memories are not tangible things. "He had his Mona. She's still waiting for him. She doesn't know anything about what's happened here. Who's going to tell her, Kyle? You'd better kill me and then ride to Palo Pinto and tell her you made a clean sweep of things. Kill me, Kyle, or I'm killing you."

"I've got the drop on you, Steve," said Reeve, beginning to breathe a trifle fast. His chest rose and fell perceptibly. "You can't do a thing as long as I've got the drop on you."

"If you don't kill me now, I'll trail you. I promise you that, Kyle. I'll trail you to hell and back and I'll kill you someday. So you'd better kill me now."

Slowly, Reeve rose to his feet. His face had paled. He had taken on an expression of considering something profound, something akin to the searching of his own soul for all the good and evil he had ever done. For a moment everything in his bearing suggested that he was striving for a decision. When he reached it, his face turned gray.

"All right," he said, and his voice was calm and sad, but also hard. "I know you. You'll hound me the rest of your days. I can run, but you'd hound me. Well, I won't live like that. I've told you my side of it. I've told it to you exactly as it was. If you think I did in Eddie and the Hepburn kid, go on and kill me. You won't even have to hound me. You can kill me now."

He threw the .45 at Britton's feet.

The surprise of it stunned Britton and for a moment he just crouched there, staring wide-eyed at the gun in front of him. Then a burst of rage and vile exhilaration rushed to his brain. He grabbed the gun and brought it up, his lips curling back from his teeth, every fiber in him aquiver with wrath and hate.

Carmen cried out. As Britton racked back the hammer and leveled the .45, she jumped in front of Reeve. She spread her arms as though to encircle him behind her. Her distraught face worked convulsively, her eyes glimmered with a frenzied, terror-stricken light.

"No, Steve, no," she screamed.

"Get out of the way, Carmen," snarled Britton, finger curled tightly around the trigger.

"But why? Why?"

"You know why. Get out of the way."

"You can't blame him for Eddie."

"Can't I?" he snarled. Rage and hate lashed him, something brutal and malevolent was shrieking in his brain. "I'll show you if I can't. Stand away from him."

"If you're going to blame anyone for Eddie," she cried, "blame me. It was because of me that Kyle got mad at you. Blame me," she cried, tears streaking her cheeks. "As long as you're looking at it in such a twisted, crazy way, blame me. Kill me then."

The bearded cast of his face remained stern and implacable. His mind could see only the one cruel thing. "Stand aside, Carmen," he shouted. "Damn you, stand aside!"

"I won't stand aside," she sobbed. "You'll have to kill me if you want to kill Kyle. I'm to blame and so are you. You're to blame as much as me. It was you and me together that got Kyle mad. If you're going to blame anyone for Eddie, blame yourself. After all, I was Kyle's wife."

The import of this stunned Britton. He had never looked at it in that light. The heedless ire died in him. Reason returned and with it came remorse and the chilling realization of how close he had come to doing something that he would have grieved for the rest of his life.

The .45 sagged in his hand. Carmen saw and her head dropped and she covered her face with the palms of her hands and began to sob hoarsely. Reeve put an arm around her and drew her tenderly against him. His hand caressed her hair and above Carmen's head his eyes watched Britton.

Britton opened his hand and the .45 made a soft

plop as it hit the ground. Slowly, Britton came up on his feet. His knees seemed so weak that they could hardly support him, the muscles of his thighs were fluttering in reaction.

He went over and picked up his gun belt and strapped it on. Then he picked up his Winchester and went up to the corral and got his black. Reeve and Carmen were still standing there, arms about each other, as Britton rode past. He did not so much as glance at them.

The black moved on. Britton lifted it into a trot as he passed through the canyon's mouth. The black's hoofs kicked up small puffs of dust that were quickly gone. . . .

15

He picked up Rambone's trail on the other side of the Ladrones. A cowpuncher riding fence had seen Rambone passing by and this was the first trace Britton gathered of the former Chain Link ramrod.

Rambone swung south. The border was a good three hundred miles away, but this appeared to be his destination. His trail never varied. His tracks moved ever southward, avoiding towns and even tiny settlements. Rambone picked up his supplies at isolated ranches and moved on.

Britton followed with a doggedness and single-mindedness that gaunted his cheeks and sweated the last bit of suet out of his frame. He had stopped shaving and the black whiskers rimmed his mouth and covered the planes of his face and the front of his neck. The whiskers concealed any expression he might have worn, but they could not hide the glint of naked savagery in his eyes.

The blaze-faced black played out and Britton swapped it for a bay with white stockings. He hated parting with the black, but sentiment did not hold much with Britton these days. The hate and purpose were too deep and malevolent. He gave the black a slap on the neck and then he mounted the bay and rode on.

He thought now and then of Stella, usually in those moments at night before dropping off in exhausted slumber. At times the recollections were quite poignant, they started a small, sad wailing in his heart. Other times the memories seemed distant and unreal. They paraded before his eyes like the confused remnants of a troubled dream.

He never dwelt on the future except that he would try to get Rambone. Britton's mind planned nothing else. After all, he had no assurance that he would come out of this alive and so he saw nothing but folly in building another dream. Only the future held the answer to that.

There were nights when he would come suddenly awake, sitting bolt upright in his blankets, aware that he had shouted something, but never remembering that he had cried Stella's name. He would sit like that awhile, seeking to recall something of that which had awakened him, but recollection never came. Finally, he would lie down again and, in time, fall asleep once more.

In due time, Rambone became aware that he was being followed. The first realization Britton had of this was when he came across a water hole that had been deliberately muddied by riding a horse again and again through it. This was yucca country, desolate and arid, with heat waves shimmering over the land and dancing in beguiling convolutions against the backdrop of the distant mountains. With so little water available, Britton had to wait until most of the grime had settled before filling his canteens and riding on.

One day he thought he caught a glimpse of a horseman topping a distant ridge, but the point was so far off and then the heat waves had a way of tricking a man's eyes so that Britton was not sure that he had actually seen anything. He quickened the pace of the bay, but when he had gained the crest of the ridge and gazed out over the barren land ahead he saw nothing but the twisted, thorny shapes of the yucca.

Yet he knew Rambone was out there. He knew this because every water hole he came across had been recently muddied. This was Rambone's way of slowing down Britton and giving him nothing but brackish water to drink. Nevertheless, Britton rode on.

The day he came across the spring that had been left untouched Britton's mind held nothing but the joyful knowledge that he was going to taste cool, clean water again. He could see where some-one had lain on the sandy ground while drinking and then the tracks of a horse going away, heading south. These were the only facts that Britton considered. He dismounted and, dropping on his belly beside the bay, drank thirstily.

It was the bay who sensed it first. The horse's

ears pricked up and then its head whipped up suddenly and even as this was going on it abruptly dawned on Britton what was under way and without waiting for more he began to roll as fast as he could. The whip of the shot was a flat crack that split the silence. Something kicked dirt over Britton's shirt and he kept right on rolling as another shot rang out.

The bay squealed with fright and wheeled away. Its front feet stepped on the trailing lines and jerked its head down. It stopped and then shied again at the sound of the second shot and again trampled the lines and stood there, snorting and trumpeting its fear and consternation.

The third shot chipped slivers off the stone behind which Britton rolled. He came to a stop there, breathing fast and hard, sweat starting to trickle down through the tangle of whiskers on his cheeks. He lay there, motionless except for the heaving of his chest, listening while another slug ricocheted off the rock and shrieked off across the land.

Then the gun grew silent and Britton lay there thinking. It was obvious what Rambone had done. He had planned and executed this cleverly. Leaving the spring undisturbed, he had ridden on, then doubled back and taken up a position among the rocks on the slope above the spring and waited for Britton. It was only a stroke of luck that Britton had escaped unscratched. Now he was in a fix, pinned down here behind this rock with only his .44 because his Winchester was in the saddle boot on the bay. Rambone had both his six-shooter and rifle.

Britton lay there quietly until his breathing was calm and even again. He had lost his hat and in rolling and sliding he had rent the side of his shirt. He drew his .44 and inserted a cartridge in the sixth chamber which he usually carried empty under the hammer. Then he waited, thinking.

He got a brief, searing vision of a body swinging in the wind and a sob almost tore out of him. I've failed you, Eddie, he thought anguishedly and miserably. Like a damn fool I've let him pin me down. Who's going to square for you if he gets me?

He went on thinking and nothing came to him, only the mournful memory of a song.

"As I walked out in the streets of Laredo,
As I walked out in Laredo one day,
I spied a poor cowboy wrapped up in white
  linen,
Wrapped up in white linen and cold as the
  clay . . ."

He closed his eyes and cursed bitterly and tried shutting his ears but the song went on, tantalizing him with its phantasmal insistence. His eyes stung. Wrath and hate and frustration made him curse again.

" 'I see by your outfit that you are a cowboy,'
These words he did say as I boldly stepped by.
'Come sit down beside me and hear my sad
  story;
I was shot in the breast and I know I must
  die . . .' "

He decided to take a look around and he rose up slowly and cautiously, but the instant the tip of his head showed above the boulder something whined piercingly and shards of stone stung his cheeks and as he was going down the crack of the shot struck his ears. Rambone tried another bullet that chipped off more bits of rock. When the echoes of this shot had faded away, there was only the awesome, portentous silence of the abandoned land.

" 'Let sixteen gamblers come handle my
  coffin,
Let sixteen cowboys come sing me a song,
Take me to the graveyard and lay the sod o'er
  me,
For I'm a poor cowboy and I know I've done
  wrong . . .' "

Sweat dampened Britton's beard, sweat trickled down into his eyes and he drew the back of a hand across them wiping them dry, but almost instantly they were wet with sweat again. He

cursed half aloud, viciously, bitterly, almost sobbing with rage and helplessness. Eddie, he
thought. I've let you down, Eddie. . . .

> " 'It was once in the saddle I used to go
>   dashing,
> It was once in the saddle I used to go gay.
> 'Twas first to drinking and then to card
>   playing,
> Got shot in the breast, I am dying today . . .' "

He turned on his side and for a long time
contemplated a group of brown boulders
arranged in the shape of a mound. They were off
to his right about twenty feet away and between
him and the mound the yucca grew in profusion.
Nevertheless, it would not afford much protec-
tion and he felt his throat go dry and the palms of
his hands tingle as he reached his decision. He
might not make it, he realized, and he had an
aching vision of Stella that left him strangely sad
and spent inside.

> " 'Get six jolly cowboys to carry my coffin,
> Get six pretty girls to carry my pall;
> Put bunches of roses all over my coffin,
> Put roses to deaden the clods as they fall . . .' "

He gathered himself, crouching, and then he
darted out, running as swiftly as he could bent

over. Rambone was caught by surprise. His first shot was slow in coming and then it snipped thorns off a yucca next to Britton's head. Rambone's gun roared again and along with the sound something plucked at Britton's sleeve. He threw himself forward as the rifle blasted a third time and this slug cut a furrow along Britton's back and then he was crawling and scrambling in the sand. The next slug kicked a mouthful of dust into his face and then he had reached the shelter of the mound and lay there, flat on his belly, spitting dust and blinking grit out of his eyes.

" 'Oh beat the drum slowly and play the fife lowly
And play the dead march as you carry me along,
Take me to the green valley and lay the sod o'er me,
For I'm a young cowboy and I know I've done wrong . . .' "

As soon as his eyes had cleared, Britton circled the mound. The land rose here. Crags and slivers of rock littered the slope and he went up among these, moving as fast as he could. Rambone spied him a couple of times and slugs came whistling up at Britton, but each time he got behind a crag and the bullets just ricocheted harmlessly off stone. Then Rambone's gun was silent.

Britton ventured a look for he was above

Rambone now and he saw the man coming out from his boulders. Britton fired down, but Rambone dived behind a stone and the slug missed. Britton crouched there, hugging the rough surface of a large slab, peering down. He got another glimpse of Rambone moving off and up as he sought to get above Britton again. Britton fired a shot, but this one missed too. He punched out the spent shells and reloaded.

He was thinking that Rambone was still carrying his rifle and this gave him the edge for he could shoot from long range. He could not allow Rambone to get too far away. He had to keep Rambone within six-shooter range.

Britton left the shelter of the slab and slid down between two huge stones with a space between them just large enough for him to squeeze through. He ran along the foot of a ledge with an overhang that cut him off from view above. He emerged at the end of this into the open and, glancing up, he saw Rambone, preparing to leap from one crag to another.

Rambone spied Britton at the same time and Rambone checked his progress so abruptly that he teetered and almost fell. His face slacked with surprise and consternation. He recovered himself and steadied and started to bring the rifle to his shoulder.

Britton fired. The slug smashed up into Rambone's chest and ripped a hoarse, loud cry of pain out of him. The rifle dropped from his grip, bounced off stone and fell, winking in the sun, almost at Britton's feet.

Britton fired again. This slug drove Rambone back. His foot started to slip, but in desperation he threw himself forward and down. Britton fired once more. This slug tagged Rambone before he touched the top of the next crag. The pain of it convulsed him. His body arched and twisted side-ways in a spasm of anguish and then he was over the lip of the crag and falling.

He fell with his arms and legs thrashing and a puff of dust rose where he hit the ground. He was still breathing when Britton walked up to him, but Rambone did not have long to go. The whites of his eyes were showing and a trickle of blood dribbled out of one corner of his gaping, gasping mouth and there was a rattle in each labored pant. His fingers opened and closed aimlessly and he kept arching his left knee.

Britton stood, breathing hard, the .44 still gripped in his hand. In the seventy-two years that Steve Britton lived, this was the only time he enjoyed watching a man die. . . .

He returned to the Ladrones with fall in the wind. The grass in the meadows and on the slopes was brown and sere, only the pines and junipers were still green. There was the sad air of dying about everything.

He had not wanted to return here, not to this part of the Ladrones, not to where his dream had started to take tangible shape before shattering beyond reclamation. He kept telling himself that he should have gone to Chain Link or, better yet, to Cordova and then sent for Stella and, if she was still willing, gone away with her. He should never have come here to the canyon.

Yet something drew him, something sweet and sad and compelling. He could not resist it.

He had finally shaved off the whiskers the night before and his face looked strange, a deep brown that was almost black on the forehead and around the eyes and grayly pale where the beard had covered his features. Staring into the mirror, he had noticed how gaunt his cheeks had grown; the hollows were very pronounced. The wrinkles had increased at the edges of his eyes and the bitter twist of his mouth was more marked than ever.

He could not shake the bitterness from him. All his mind would hold was the fact that he had nothing to offer Stella.

As he rode through the canyon's mouth, the faint neighing of a horse reached him. The bay pricked up its ears and answered. Britton reined in, heart quickening, something cloying filling his throat. A moment he was like that, then he touched the bay with the spurs and rode in at a gallop.

He could hardly believe it when his eyes saw it. The corrals held mustangs, not as many as they once had held, but they were not empty as they had been the last time he had seen them. Kyle Reeve, covered with dust and grime and sweating profusely, came out of the breaking corral. He grinned when he looked at Britton and then Reeve stood there, seeming awkward and even uncomfortable. Carmen came out of the corral now, brushing dust from her Levi's. She smiled shyly when she glanced at Britton.

Reeve spread his hands and then, realizing that the gesture explained nothing, he said, "Hell, Steve, this is the least we could do. Me and Carmen. We'll get your horses back and you won't have to cut us in for anything. We knew you'd be back. We never doubted you'd be back. So we've been here working. Me and Carmen and Stella. She's helped us too."

"Stella?" cried Britton. His voice was hoarse, he hardly recognized it as his own.

"Sure," grinned Reeve. "Didn't you see her when you rode past the camp?"

Britton heard her call his name then and he stepped down hurriedly from the bay and turned and there she was, running toward him. He saw her only vaguely through the mist that suddenly dimmed his eyes. Then she was in his arms, face buried against his neck, sobbing and quivering.

"Steve, Steve," she sobbed, every word a

caress in his ears. "I worried so much for you, Steve. I cried every night for you. I cried because I was sad and lonely and feared for you. I cried because I thought I would never see you again. I'm crying now, too, but that's because I'm happy. Do you know how it is, Steve?"

He buried his face in the silk of her hair so that the wetness in his own eyes would not show. "Sure," he whispered, throat so full that he could not speak louder. "I know. . . ."

About the Author

H(enry) A(ndrew) DeRosso was born on July 15, 1917 in Carey, Wisconsin. This area, in the northeast corner of the state near the Michigan border, is rich in its own pioneer history. Carey and its neighboring community of Hurley in which DeRosso made his home for many years were once rough-and-tumble iron-ore mining towns not unlike the gold, silver, and copper camps of the Far West frontier. This rural milieu, with its harsh winters and its proximity to the vast North Woods, may explain DeRosso's early interest in adventure and Western fiction and his lifelong fascination with the southwestern desert country, a wilderness and a climate exactly opposite of the one in which he lived. He began producing Western short stories while a high-school student, making his first professional sale to Street & Smith's *Western Story Magazine* in 1941. Health problems kept him out of military service during World War II, and thus he was able to continue writing on a daily basis and to begin piling up sales to *Western Story* and other pulps during this period, supplementing his income with farm work and as a mail carrier. By the end of the war he had established himself to the point where he was able to devote his full time to writing. Nearly all of his tales are set in the stark, desolate wastes of the Southwest. In the decades between 1940 and 1960 he published approximately two hundred Western short stories and short novels in various pulp magazines that became known for their dark and compelling visions of the night side of life and their austere realism. He was also the author of six Western novels, perhaps the most notable of which are *.44* (1953) and *End of the Gun* (1955). He died on October 14, 1960. Most recently his short stories are being collected and published, including *Under the Burning Sun* (1997) and *Riders of the Shadowlands* (1999).

Center Point Large Print
600 Brooks Road / PO Box 1
Thorndike, ME 04986-0001 USA

(207) 568-3717

US & Canada:
1 800 929-9108
www.centerpointlargeprint.com